THE SCARLET LETTER:
Easy Read Edition

Written by Nathaniel Hawthorne

Edited by Brian Burns

Published by P&L Publications

Edited by Brian Burns

Copyright 2014 by Brian Burns

ISBN – 13: 978-1497512818

ISBN-10: 1497512816

Easy Read Edition: Everything You Need in Half the Time

This edition of The Scarlet Letter is the Easy Read Edition. The book has been abridged in order to deliver the reader with everything necessary in the book to get the full experience of Hawthorne's amazing work while making it easier to read as well as less time consuming. The reader will be able to read the entire book in half the time as reading the unabridged version and yet will not miss out on anything of importance that is in the original.

For students, this book is a way to read The Scarlett Letter in a more efficient manner and still be able to pass any test that you may be given in class. In addition, study materials can be found in the back of the book and include:

- List and summary of the main characters
- Summary of Chapters: Important items from each chapter are listed in clear bulletin points
- Sample Quizzes with answers

For all readers, this book is a simple and easy way to enjoy a work of classic literature in a format that is reader friendly. You will be able to enjoy everything about the classic in less time than the original.

A note about the editing: In abridging this book, the editor has kept almost all of the original language the same. In some cases words were updated with current spelling practices and there were other sentence alterations. Sections and/or words that were not deemed pertinent to understanding the book or grasping the full importance of the book were cut out of this edition.

Table of Contents

THE CUSTOM-HOUSE

It is a little remarkable, that an autobiographical impulse should twice in my life have taken possession of me, in addressing the public. The first time was three or four years since, when I favored the reader with a description of my way of life in the deep quietude of an Old Manse. And now it will be seen that this Custom-House sketch has a certain propriety, of a kind always recognized in literature, as explaining how a large portion of the following pages came into my possession, and as offering proofs of the authenticity of a narrative therein contained. This, in fact, a desire to put myself in my true position as editor, or very little more, of the most prolix among the tales that make up my volume, this, and no other, is my true reason for assuming a personal relation with the public. In accomplishing the main purpose, it has appeared allowable, by a few extra touches, to give a faint representation of a mode of life not heretofore described, together with some of the characters that move in it, among whom the author happened to make one.

In my native town of Salem was a bustling wharf, but which is now burdened with decayed wooden warehouses, and exhibits few or no symptoms of commercial life. From the loftiest point of its roof, during precisely three and a half hours of each forenoon, floats or droops, in breeze or calm, the banner of the republic; but with the thirteen stripes turned vertically, instead of horizontally, and thus indicating that a civil, and not a military, post of Uncle Sam's government is here established. Its front is ornamented with a portico of half-a-dozen wooden pillars, supporting a balcony, beneath which a flight of wide granite steps descends towards the street. Over the entrance hovers an enormous specimen of the American eagle, with outspread wings, a shield before her breast, and, if I recollect aright, a bunch of intermingled thunderbolts and barbed arrows in each claw. With the customary infirmity of temper that characterizes this unhappy fowl, she appears by the fierceness of her beak and eye, and the general truculency of her attitude, to threaten mischief to the inoffensive community; and especially to warn all citizens careful of their safety against intruding on the premises which she overshadows with her wings. Nevertheless, vixenly as she looks, many people are seeking at this very moment to shelter themselves under the wing of the federal eagle; imagining, I presume, that her bosom has all the softness and snugness of an eiderdown pillow. But she has no great tenderness even in her best of moods, and, sooner or later is apt to fling off her nestlings with a scratch of her claw, a dab of her beak, or a rankling wound from her barbed arrows.

The pavement round about the above-described edifice, which we may as well name at once as the Custom-House of the port, has grass enough growing in its chinks to show that it has not, of late days, been worn by any multitudinous resort of business. In some months of the year, however, there often chances a forenoon when affairs move onward with a livelier tread. On some such morning, when three or four vessels happen to have arrived at once usually from Africa or South America, or to be on the verge of their departure thitherward, there is a sound of frequent feet passing briskly up and down the granite steps. Here you may greet the sea-flushed ship-master, just in port, with his vessel's papers under his arm in a tarnished tin box. Here, too, comes his owner, cheerful, somber, gracious or in the sulks, accordingly as his scheme of the now accomplished voyage has been realized in merchandise that will readily be turned to gold, or has buried him under a bulk of incommodities such as nobody will care to rid him of. Here, likewise, the germ of the wrinkle-browed, grizzly-bearded, careworn merchant, we have the smart young clerk, who gets the taste of traffic as a wolf-cub does of blood, and already sends adventures in his master's ships, when he had better be sailing mimic boats upon a mill-pond. Another figure in the scene is the outward-bound sailor, in quest of a protection; or the recently arrived one, pale and feeble, seeking a passport to the hospital. Nor must we forget the captains. Cluster all these individuals together and, for the time being, it made the Custom-House a stirring scene. More frequently, however, on ascending the steps, you would discern a row of venerable figures, sitting in old-fashioned chairs, which were tipped on their hind legs back against the wall. Oftentimes they were asleep and they were Custom-House officers.

This old town of Salem, my native place, though I have dwelt much away from it both in boyhood and maturer years, possesses a hold on my affection, the force of which I have never realized during my seasons of actual residence here. Indeed, so far as its physical aspect is concerned, with its flat, unvaried surface, covered chiefly with wooden houses, few or none of which pretend to architectural beauty, its irregularity, which is neither picturesque nor quaint, but only tame, its long and lazy street, lounging wearisomely through the whole extent of the peninsula, with Gallows Hill and New Guinea at one end, and a view of the alms-house at the other, such being the features of my native town, it would be quite as reasonable to form a sentimental attachment to a disarranged checker-board. And yet there is within me a feeling for

Old Salem, which, in lack of a better phrase, I must be content to call affection. The sentiment is probably assignable to the deep and aged roots which my family has stuck into the soil. The attachment which I speak of is the mere sensuous sympathy of dust for dust.

But the sentiment has likewise its moral quality. The figure of that first ancestor was present to my boyish imagination as far back as I can remember. It still haunts me, and induces a sort of home-feeling with the past, which I scarcely claim in reference to the present phase of the town. I seem to have a stronger claim to a residence here on account of this grave, bearded, sable-cloaked, and steeple-crowned progenitor, who came so early, with his Bible and his sword, and trode the unworn street with such a stately port, and made so large a figure, as a man of war and peace, a stronger claim than for myself, whose name is seldom heard and my face hardly known. He had all the Puritanical traits, both good and evil. He was likewise a bitter persecutor; as witness the Quakers, who have remembered him in their histories, and relate an incident of his hard severity towards a woman of their sect, which will last longer, it is to be feared, than any record of his better deeds, although these were many. I know not whether these ancestors of mine bethought themselves to repent, and ask pardon of Heaven for their cruelties; or whether they are now groaning under the heavy consequences of them in another state of being. At all events, I, the present writer, as their representative, hereby take shame upon myself for their sakes, and pray that any curse incurred by them, as I have heard, and as the dreary and unprosperous condition of the race, for many a long year back, would argue to exist, may be now and henceforth removed.

Doubtless these stern and black-browed Puritans would have thought it quite a sufficient retribution for his sins that the old trunk of the family tree should have born an idler like myself. No aim would they recognize as laudable; no success of mine would they deem otherwise than worthless, if not positively disgraceful. "What is he?" murmurs one grey shadow of my forefathers to the other. "A writer of story books! What kind of business in life?" And yet, let them scorn me as they will, strong traits of their nature have intertwined themselves with mine.

Planted deep, in the town's earliest infancy and childhood, by these energetic men, the race has ever since subsisted here Gradually, they have sunk almost out of sight; as old houses, here and there about the streets, get covered half-way to the eaves by the accumulation of new soil. This long connection of a family with one spot, as its place of birth and burial, creates a kindred between the human being and the locality, quite independent of any charm in the scenery or moral circumstances that surround him. It is not love but instinct. The new inhabitant, who came himself from a foreign land, or whose father or grandfather came, has little claim to be called a Salemite. Human nature will not flourish, any more than a potato, if it be planted and re-planted, for too long a series of generations, in the same worn-out soil. My children have had other birth-places, and, so far as their fortunes may be within my control, shall strike their roots into unaccustomed earth.

It was this strange, indolent, unjoyous attachment for my native town that brought me to fill a place in Uncle Sam's brick edifice, when I might as well, or better, have gone somewhere else. My doom was on me. It was not the first time, nor the second, that I had gone away but yet returned. So, one fine morning I ascended the flight of granite steps, with the President's commission in my pocket, and was introduced to the corps of gentlemen who were to aid me in my weighty responsibility as chief executive officer of the Custom-House.

I do not doubt at all, whether any public functionary of the United States, either in the civil or military line, has ever had such a patriarchal body of veterans under his orders as myself. The whereabouts of the Oldest Inhabitant was at once settled when I looked at them. For upwards of twenty years before this epoch, the independent position of the Collector had kept the Salem Custom-House out of the whirlpool of political vicissitude. A soldier, he stood firmly on the pedestal of his gallant services. General Miller was radically conservative; a man over whose kindly nature habit had no slight influence; attaching himself strongly to familiar faces, and with difficulty moved to change, even when change might have brought unquestionable improvement. Thus, on taking charge of my department, I found few but aged men. They were ancient sea-captains.

The greater part of my officers were Whigs. It was well for their venerable brotherhood that the new Surveyor was not a politician. Had it been otherwise, hardly a man of the old corps would have drawn the breath of official life within a month after the exterminating angel had come up the Custom-House steps. According to the received code in such matters, it would have been nothing short of duty, in a politician, to bring every one of those white heads under the axe of the guillotine. It was plain enough to discern that the old fellows dreaded some such discourtesy at my hands. It pained, and at the same time amused me, to behold the terrors that attended my advent. They knew, these excellent old persons, that, by all established rule, they ought to have given place to younger men, more orthodox in politics, and altogether fitter than themselves to serve our common Uncle. I knew it, too, but could never quite find in my heart to act upon the knowledge. Much and deservedly to my own discredit, therefore, and considerably to the detriment of my official conscience, they continued, during my incumbency, to creep about the wharves, and loiter up and down the Custom-House steps.

The discovery was soon made, I imagine, that the new Surveyor had no great harm in him. So, with lightsome hearts and the happy consciousness of being usefully employed these good old gentlemen went through the various formalities of office.

Unless people are more than commonly disagreeable, it is my foolish habit to contract a kindness for them. As most of these old Custom-House officers had good traits, and as my position in reference to them, being paternal and protective, was favorable to the growth of friendly sentiments, I soon grew to like them all. Externally, the jollity of aged men has much in common with the mirth of children; the intellect, any more than a deep sense of humor, has little to do with the matter; it is, with both, a gleam that plays upon the surface, and imparts a sunny and cheery aspect alike to the green branch and grey, moldering trunk. In one case, however, it is real sunshine; in the other, it more resembles the phosphorescent glow of decaying wood.

The father of the Custom-House, the patriarch, not only of this little squad of officials, but, I am bold to say, of the respectable body of tide-waiters all over the United States, was a certain permanent Inspector. He might truly be termed a legitimate son of the revenue system; since his sire, a Revolutionary colonel, and formerly collector of the port, had created an office for him, and appointed him to fill it, at a period of the early ages which few living men can now remember. This Inspector, when I first knew him, was a man of fourscore years. With his florid cheek, his compact figure smartly arrayed in a bright-buttoned blue coat, his brisk and vigorous step, and his hale and hearty aspect, altogether he seemed, not young, indeed, but a kind of new contrivance of Mother Nature in the shape of man, whom age and infirmity had no business to touch. Looking at him merely as an animal, and there was very little else to look at, he was a most satisfactory object. The careless security of his life in the Custom-House, on a regular income, and with but slight and infrequent apprehensions of removal, had no doubt contributed to make time pass lightly over him. The original and more potent causes, however, lay in the rare perfection of his animal nature, the moderate proportion of intellect, and the very trifling admixture of moral and spiritual ingredients. He possessed no power of thought, no depth of feeling, no troublesome sensibilities: nothing, in short, but a few commonplace instincts, which, aided by the cheerful temper which grew inevitably out of his physical well-being, did duty very respectably, and to general acceptance, in lieu of a heart.

He was, in truth, a rare phenomenon; so perfect, in one point of view; so shallow, so delusive, so impalpable such an absolute nonentity, in every other. My conclusion was that he had no soul, no heart, no mind; nothing, as I have already said, but instincts; and yet, withal, so cunningly had the few materials of his character been put together that there was no painful perception of deficiency, but, on my part, an entire contentment with what I found in him.

There is one likeness, without which my gallery of Custom-House portraits would be strangely incomplete. It is that of the Collector, our gallant old General, who, after his brilliant military service had come hither, twenty years before, to spend the decline of his varied and honorable life. The brave soldier had already numbered, nearly or quite, his three-score years and ten, and was pursuing the remainder of his earthly march, burdened with infirmities which even the martial music of his own spirit-stirring recollections could do little towards lightening. It was only with the assistance of a servant, and by leaning his hand heavily on the iron balustrade, that he could slowly and painfully ascend the Custom-House steps, and, with a toilsome progress across the floor, attain his customary chair beside the fireplace. If his notice was sought, an expression of courtesy and interest gleamed out upon his features, proving that there was light within him, and that it was only the outward medium of the intellectual lamp that obstructed the rays in their passage. When no longer called upon to speak or listen, either of which operations cost him an evident effort, his face would briefly subside into its former not uncheerful quietude. The framework of his nature, originally strong and massive, was not yet crumpled into ruin.

Looking at the old warrior with affection, I could discern the main points of his portrait. It was marked with the noble and heroic qualities which showed it to be not a mere accident, but of good right, that he had won a distinguished name. The heat that had formerly pervaded his nature, and which was not yet extinct, was never of the kind that flashes and flickers in a blaze; but rather a deep red glow, as of iron in a furnace. Weight, solidity, firmness; this was the expression of his repose, even in such decay as had crept untimely over him at the period of which I speak. But I could imagine, even then, that, under some excitement which should go deeply into his consciousness he was yet capable of flinging off his infirmities like a sick man's gown, dropping the staff of age to seize a battle-sword, and starting up once more a warrior. And, in so intense a moment his demeanor would have still been calm. What I saw in him were the features of stubborn and ponderous endurance, which might well have amounted to obstinacy in his earlier days; of integrity, that, like most of his other endowments, lay in a somewhat heavy mass, and was just as unmalleable or unmanageable as a ton of iron ore; and of benevolence.

Many characteristics must have vanished, or been obscured, before I met the General. All merely graceful attributes are usually the most evanescent; nor does Nature adorn the human ruin with blossoms of new beauty. Still, even in respect of grace and beauty, there were points well worth noting. A trait of native elegance was shown in the General's fondness for the sight and fragrance of flowers. Here was one who seemed to have a young girl's appreciation of the floral tribe.

Literature, its exertions and objects, were now of little moment in my regard. I cared not at this period for books; they were apart from me. Nature, except it were human nature, the nature that is developed in earth and sky, was, in one sense, hidden from me; and all the imaginative delight wherewith it had been spiritualized passed away out of my mind. A gift, a faculty, if it had not been departed, was suspended and inanimate within me.

Meanwhile, there I was, a Surveyor of the Revenue and, so far as I have been able to understand, as good a Surveyor as need be. My fellow-officers, and the merchants and sea-captains with whom my official duties brought me into any manner of connection, viewed me in no other light, and probably knew me in no other character. None of them, I presume, had ever read a page of my indicting, or would have cared a fig the more for me if they had read them all; nor would it have mended the matter, in the least, had those same unprofitable pages been written with a pen like that of Burns or of Chaucer, each of whom was a Custom-House officer in his day, as well as I.

No longer seeking nor caring that my name should be blazoned abroad on title-pages, I smiled to think that it had now another kind of vogue. The Custom-House marker imprinted it, with a stencil and black paint, on pepper-bags, and baskets of anatto, and cigar-boxes, and bales of all kinds of dutiable merchandise, in testimony that these commodities had paid the impost, and gone regularly through the office. Borne on such queer vehicle of fame, a knowledge of my existence, so far as a name conveys it, was carried where it had never been before, and, I hope, will never go again.

But the past was not dead. Once in a great while, the thoughts that had seemed so vital and so active, yet had been put to rest so quietly, revived again. One of the most remarkable occasions was that which brings it within the law of literary propriety to offer the public the sketch which I am now writing.

In the second story of the Custom-House there is a large room, in which the brick-work and naked rafters have never been covered with paneling and plaster. The edifice contains far more space than its occupants know what to do with. At one end of the room, in a recess, were a number of barrels piled one upon another, containing bundles of official documents. Here, no doubt, statistics of the former commerce of Salem might be discovered, and memorials of her princely merchants, old King Derby, old Billy Gray, old Simon Forrester, and many another magnate in his day. The founders of the greater part of the families which now compose the aristocracy of Salem might here be traced, from the petty and obscure beginnings of their traffic, at periods generally much posterior to the Revolution, upward to what their children look upon as long-established rank.

Prior to the Revolution there is a dearth of records; the earlier documents and archives of the Custom-House having, probably, been carried off to Halifax, when all the king's officials accompanied the British army in its flight from Boston.

But, one idle and rainy day, it was my fortune to make a discovery of some little interest. Poking and burrowing into the heaped-up rubbish in the corner, unfolding one and another document, I chanced to lay my hand on a small package, carefully done up in a piece of ancient yellow parchment. This envelope had the air of an official record of some period long past. There was something about it that quickened an instinctive curiosity, and made me undo the faded red tape that tied up the package, with the sense that a treasure would here be brought to light. I found it to be a commission, under the hand and seal of Governor Shirley, in favor of one Jonathan Pue, as Surveyor of His Majesty's Customs for the Port of Salem, in the Province of Massachusetts Bay. I remembered to have read a notice of the decease of Mr. Surveyor Pue, about fourscore years ago.

They were documents, in short, not official, but of a private nature. I could account for their being included in the heap of Custom-House lumber only by the fact that Mr. Pue's death had happened suddenly, and that these papers, which he probably kept in his official desk, had never come to the knowledge of his heirs, or were supposed to relate to the business of the revenue.

The object that most drew my attention to the mysterious package was a certain affair of fine red cloth, much worn and faded,

There were traces about it of gold embroidery, which, however, was greatly frayed and defaced, so that none, or very little, of the glitter was left. This rag of scarlet cloth, on careful examination, assumed the shape of a letter. It was the capital letter A. Certainly there was some deep meaning in it most worthy of interpretation, and which, as it were, streamed forth from the mystic symbol, subtly communicating itself to my sensibilities, but evading the analysis of my mind.

While thus perplexed, I happened to place it on my breast. It seemed to me, the reader may smile, but must not doubt my word, it seemed to me, then, that I experienced a sensation not altogether physical, yet almost so, as of burning heat, and as if the letter were not of red cloth, but red-hot iron. I shuddered, and involuntarily let it fall upon the floor.

In the absorbing contemplation of the scarlet letter, I had neglected to examine a small roll of dingy paper, around which it had been twisted. This I now opened, and had the satisfaction to find recorded by the old Surveyor's pen, a reasonably complete explanation of the whole affair. There were several foolscap sheets, containing many particulars respecting the life and conversation of one Hester Prynne, who appeared to have been rather a noteworthy personage in the view of our ancestors. Prying further into the manuscript, I found the record of other doings and sufferings of this singular woman, for most of which the reader is referred to the story entitled "The Scarlet Letter"; and it should be borne carefully in mind that the main facts of that story are authorized and authenticated by the document of Mr. Surveyor Pue. The original papers, together with the scarlet letter itself, are still in my possession, and shall be freely exhibited to whomsoever may desire a sight of them. I must not be understood affirming that, in the dressing up of the tale, I have invariably confined myself within the limits of the old Surveyor's half-a-dozen sheets of foolscap. On the contrary, I have allowed myself, as to such points, nearly, or altogether, as much license as if the facts had been entirely of my own invention. What I contend for is the authenticity of the outline.

This incident recalled my mind, in some degree, to its old track. There seemed to be here the groundwork of a tale. It impressed me as if the ancient Surveyor, in his garb of a hundred years gone by, and wearing his immortal wig, had met me in the deserted chamber of the Custom-House.

On Hester Prynne's story, therefore, I bestowed much thought. It was the subject of my meditations for many an hour, while pacing to and fro across my room, or traversing, with a hundredfold repetition, the long extent from the front door of the Custom-House to the side entrance, and back again. I doubt whether the tale of "The Scarlet Letter" would ever have been brought before the public eye. My imagination was a tarnished mirror. It would not reflect, or only with miserable dimness, the figures with which I did my best to people it. The characters of the narrative would not be warmed and rendered malleable by any heat that I could kindle at my intellectual forge.

It was not merely during the three hours and a half which Uncle Sam claimed as his share of my daily life that this wretched numbness held possession of me. It went with me on my sea-shore walks and rambles into the country. Nor did it quit me when, late at night, I sat in the deserted parlor, lighted only by the glimmering coal-fire and the moon, striving to picture forth imaginary scenes, which, the next day, might flow out on the brightening page in many-hued description.

At the Instant, I was only conscious that what would have been a pleasure once was now a hopeless toil. I had ceased to be a writer of tolerably poor tales and essays, and had become a tolerably good Surveyor of the Customs. That was all. But, nevertheless, it is anything but agreeable to be haunted by a suspicion that one's intellect is dwindling away, or exhaling, without your consciousness, so that, at every glance, you find a smaller and less volatile residuum.
Here was a fine prospect in the distance. I began to grow melancholy and restless; continually prying into my mind, to discover which of its poor properties were gone, and what degree of detriment had already accrued to the remainder. I endeavored to calculate how much longer I could stay in the Custom-House, and yet go forth a man. I was likely to grow grey and decrepit in the Surveyorship, and become much such another animal as the old Inspector. But, all this while, I was giving myself very unnecessary alarm. Providence had meditated better things for me than I could possibly imagine for myself.

A remarkable event of the third year of my Surveyorship-to adopt the tone of "P. P. "-was the election of General Taylor to the Presidency. It is essential, in order to form a complete estimate of the advantages of official life, to view the incumbent at the in-coming of a hostile administration. His position is then one of the most singularly irksome, and, in every contingency, disagreeable, that a wretched mortal can possibly occupy. But it is a strange experience, to a man of pride and sensibility, to know that his interests are within the control of individuals who neither love nor understand him. The Democrats take the offices, as a general rule, because they need them, and because the practice of many years has made it the law of political warfare, which unless a different system be proclaimed, it was weakness and cowardice to murmur at.

I saw much reason to congratulate myself that I was on the losing side rather than the triumphant one. I saw my own prospect of retaining office to be better than those of my democratic brethren. But who can see an inch into futurity beyond his nose? My own head was the first that fell!

The moment when a man's head drops off is seldom or never, I am inclined to think, precisely the most agreeable of his life. Nevertheless, like the greater part of our misfortunes, even so serious a contingency brings its remedy and consolation with it, if the sufferer will but make the best rather than the worst, of the accident which has befallen him. I had spent three years; a term long enough to rest a weary brain: long enough to break off old intellectual habits, and make room for new ones: long enough, and too long, to have lived in an unnatural state, doing what was really of no advantage nor delight to any human being, and withholding myself from toil that would, at least, have stilled an unquiet impulse in me.

So much for my figurative self. The real human being all this time, with his head safely on his shoulders, had brought himself to the comfortable conclusion that everything was for the best; and making an investment in ink, paper, and steel pens, had opened his long-disused writing desk, and was again a literary man.

Now it was that the lucubrations of my ancient predecessor, Mr. Surveyor Pue, came into play. Rusty through long idleness, some little space was requisite before my intellectual machinery could be brought to work upon the tale with an effect in any degree satisfactory. Even yet, though my thoughts were ultimately much absorbed in the task, it wears, to my eye, a stern and somber aspect: too much ungladdened by genial sunshine; too little relieved by the tender and familiar influences which soften almost every scene of nature and real life, and undoubtedly should soften every picture of them.

The life of the Custom-House lies like a dream behind me. Henceforth it ceases to be a reality of my life; I am a citizen of somewhere else. I shall do better amongst other faces; and these familiar ones, it need hardly be said, will do just as well without me.

It may be, however, oh, transporting and triumphant thought, that the great-grandchildren of the present race may sometimes think kindly of the scribbler of bygone days, when the antiquary of days to come, among the sites memorable in the town's history, shall point out the locality of the town pump.

CHAPTER 1: THE PRISON DOOR

A throng of bearded men, in sad-colored garments and grey steeple-crowned hats, inter-mixed with women, was assembled in front of a wooden edifice, the door of which was heavily timbered with oak, and studded with iron spikes.

The founders of a new colony recognized it among their earliest practical necessities to allot a portion of the virgin soil as a cemetery, and another portion as the site of a prison. In accordance with this rule it may safely be assumed that the forefathers of Boston had built the first prison-house somewhere in the Vicinity of Cornhill. Certain it is that, some fifteen or twenty years after the settlement of the town, the wooden jail was already marked with weather-stains and other indications of age, which gave a yet darker aspect to its beetle-browed and gloomy front. Like all that pertains to crime, it seemed never to have known a youthful era. Before this ugly edifice was a grass-plot, much overgrown with unsightly vegetation. But, on one side of the portal was a wild rose-bush, covered, in this month of June, with its delicate gems, which might be imagined to offer their fragrance and fragile beauty to the prisoner as he went in, and to the condemned criminal as he came forth to his doom, in token that the deep heart of Nature could pity and be kind to him.

Finding it so directly on the threshold of our narrative, which is now about to issue from that inauspicious portal, we could hardly do otherwise than pluck one of its flowers, and present it to the reader. It may serve, let us hope, to symbolize some sweet moral blossom that may be found along the track, or relieve the darkening close of a tale of human frailty and sorrow.

CHAPTER 2: THE MARKET-PLACE

The grass-plot before the jail, in Prison Lane was occupied by a large number of the inhabitants of Boston, all with their eyes intently fastened on the iron-clamped oaken door. There was a solemnity of demeanor on the part of the spectators, as befitted a people among whom religion and law were almost identical, and in whose character both were so thoroughly interfused, that the mildest and severest acts of public discipline were alike made venerable and awful. On the other hand, a penalty which, in our days, would infer a degree of mocking infamy and ridicule, might then be invested with almost as stern a dignity as the punishment of death itself.

It was a circumstance to be noted on the summer morning when our story begins its course, that the women appeared to take a peculiar interest in whatever penal infliction might be expected to ensue. Morally, as well as materially, there was a coarser fiber in those wives and maidens of old English birth and breeding than in their fair descendants. The women who were now standing about the prison-door stood within less than half a century of the period when the man-like Elizabeth had been the not altogether unsuitable representative of the sex. They were her countrywomen. The bright morning sun, therefore, shone on broad shoulders and well-developed busts, and on round and ruddy cheeks. There was, moreover, a boldness and rotundity of speech among these matrons that would startle us at the present day, whether in respect to its purport or its volume of tone.

"Goodwives," said a hard-featured dame of fifty, "It would be greatly for the public behoove if we women should have the handling of such malefactresses as this Hester Prynne. What think ye, gossips? If the hussy stood up for judgment before us five would she come off with such a sentence as the worshipful magistrates have awarded? Marry, I think not."

"People say," said another, "that the Reverend Master Dimmesdale, her godly pastor, takes it very grievously to heart that such a scandal should have come upon his congregation."

"The magistrates are God-fearing gentlemen, but merciful overmuch, that is a truth," added a third autumnal matron. "At the very least, they should have put the brand of a hot iron on Hester Prynne's forehead."

"Ah, but," interposed, more softly, a young wife, holding a child by the hand, "let her cover the mark as she will, the pang of it will be always in her heart."

"What do we talk of marks and brands, whether on the bodice of her gown or the flesh of her forehead?" cried another female, the ugliest of these self-constituted judges. "This woman has brought shame upon us all, and ought to die; is there not law for it? Truly there is, both in the Scripture and the statute-book."

The door of the jail being flung open from within there appeared, in the first place, the grim and gristly presence of the town-beadle. Stretching forth the official staff in his left hand, he laid his right upon the shoulder of a young woman, whom he thus drew forward, until, on the threshold of the prison-door, she repelled him, by an action marked with natural dignity and force of character, and stepped into the open air as if by her own free will. She bore in her arms a child, a baby of some three months old, who winked and turned aside its little face from the too vivid light of day; because its existence, heretofore, had brought it acquaintance only with the grey twilight of a dungeon, or other darksome apartment of the prison.

When the young woman stood fully revealed before the crowd, it seemed to be her first impulse to clasp the infant closely to her bosom; not so much by an impulse of motherly affection, as that she might thereby conceal a certain token, which was wrought or fastened into her dress. In a moment, however, wisely judging that one token of her shame would but poorly serve to hide another, she took the baby on her arm, and with a burning blush, and yet a haughty smile, looked around at her townspeople and neighbors. On the breast of her gown, in fine red cloth, surrounded with an elaborate embroidery and fantastic flourishes of gold thread, appeared the letter A.

The young woman was tall, with a figure of perfect elegance on a large scale. She had dark and abundant hair, so glossy that it threw off the sunshine with a gleam; and a face which, besides being beautiful from regularity of feature and richness of complexion, had the impressiveness belonging to a marked brow and deep black eyes. Her attire seemed to express the attitude of her spirit, the desperate recklessness of her mood, by its wild and picturesque peculiarity. But the point which drew all eyes was that scarlet letter, so fantastically embroidered and illuminated upon her bosom. It had the effect of a spell, taking her out of the ordinary relations with humanity, and enclosing her in a sphere by herself.

"It were well," muttered the most iron-visaged of the old dames, "if we stripped Madame Hester's rich gown off her dainty shoulders; and as for the red letter which she hath stitched so curiously, I'll bestow a rag of mine own rheumatic flannel to make a fitter one!"

"Oh, peace, neighbors, peace!" whispered their youngest companion; "do not let her hear you! Not a stitch in that embroidered letter but she has felt it in her heart."

The grim beadle now made a gesture with his staff. "Make way, good people, make way, in the King's name!" cried he. "Open a passage. Come along, Madame Hester, and show your scarlet letter in the market-place!"

A lane was forthwith opened through the crowd of spectators. Hester Prynne set forth towards the place appointed for her punishment. It was no great distance, in those days, from the prison door to the market-place. Measured by the prisoner's experience, however, it might be reckoned a journey of some length. In our nature, however, there is a provision that the sufferer should never know the intensity of what he endures by its present torture but chiefly by the pang that rankles after it. With almost a serene deportment, therefore, Hester Prynne passed through this portion of her ordeal, and came to a sort of scaffold, at the western extremity of the market-place.

In fact, this scaffold constituted a portion of a penal machine. It was, in short, the platform of the pillory; and above it rose the framework of that instrument of discipline, so fashioned as to confine the human head in its tight grasp, and thus hold it up to the public gaze. In Hester Prynne's instance, however, as not infrequently in other cases, her sentence bore that she should stand a certain time upon the platform, but without undergoing that gripe about the neck and confinement of the head, the proneness to which was the most devilish characteristic of this ugly engine. Knowing well her part, she ascended a flight of wooden steps, and was thus displayed to the surrounding multitude, at about the height of a man's shoulders above the street.

Had there been a Papist among the crowd of Puritans, he might have seen in this beautiful woman, so picturesque in her attire and mien, and with the infant at her bosom, an object to remind him of the image of Divine Maternity, which so many illustrious painters have vied with one another to represent; something which should remind him, indeed, but only by contrast, of that sacred image of sinless motherhood, whose infant was to redeem the world. Here, there was the taint of deepest sin in the most sacred quality of human life, working such effect, that the world was only the darker for this woman's beauty, and the more lost for the infant that she had borne.

The crowd was somber and grave. The unhappy culprit sustained herself as best a woman might, under the heavy weight of a thousand unrelenting eyes, all fastened upon her, and concentrated at her bosom. It was almost intolerable to be borne. Had a roar of laughter burst from the multitude, each man, each woman, each little shrill-voiced child, contributing their individual parts, Hester Prynne might have repaid them all with a bitter and disdainful smile. But, under the leaden infliction which it was her doom to endure, she felt, at moments, as if she must needs shriek out with the full power of her lungs, and cast herself from the scaffold down upon the ground, or else go mad at once.

Yet there were intervals when the whole scene seemed to vanish from her eyes, or, at least, glimmered indistinctly before them, like a mass of imperfectly shaped and spectral images. Her mind, and especially her memory, was preternaturally active, and kept bringing up other scenes than this roughly hewn street of a little town. Reminiscences, the most trifling and immaterial, passages of infancy and school-days, sports, childish quarrels, and the little domestic traits of her maiden years, came swarming back upon her, intermingled with recollections of whatever was gravest in her subsequent life. Possibly, it was an instinctive device of her spirit to relieve itself by the exhibition of these phantasmagoric forms, from the cruel weight and hardness of the reality.

Be that as it might, the scaffold of the pillory was a point of view that revealed to Hester Prynne the entire track along which she had been treading, since her happy infancy. Standing on that miserable eminence, she saw again her native village, in Old England, and her paternal home. She saw her father's face, with its bold brow, and reverend white beard; her mother's, too, with the look of heedful and anxious love which it always wore in her remembrance. She saw her own face, glowing with girlish beauty, and illuminating all the interior of the dusky mirror in which she had been wont to gaze at it. There she beheld another countenance, of a man well stricken in years, a pale, thin, scholar-like visage, with eyes dim and bleared by the lamp-light that had served them to pore over many ponderous books. This figure of the study and the cloister, as Hester Prynne's womanly fancy failed not to recall, was slightly deformed, with the left shoulder a trifle higher than the right. Lastly, in lieu of these shifting scenes, came back the rude market-place of the Puritan, settlement, with all the townspeople assembled, and leveling their stern regards at herself who stood on the scaffold of the pillory, an infant on her arm, and the letter A, in scarlet, fantastically embroidered with gold thread, upon her bosom.

Could it be true? She clutched the child so fiercely to her breast that it sent forth a cry; she turned her eyes downward at the scarlet letter, and even touched it with her finger, to assure herself that the infant and the shame were real. Yes these were her realities; all else had vanished!

CHAPTER 3: THE RECOGNITION

From this intense consciousness of being the object of severe and universal observation, the wearer of the scarlet letter was at length relieved, by discerning, on the outskirts of the crowd, a figure which irresistibly took possession of her thoughts. An Indian in his native garb was standing there. By the Indian's side, and evidently sustaining a companionship with him, stood a white man, clad in a strange disarray of civilized and savage costume.

He was small in stature. There was a remarkable intelligence in his features. It was evident to Hester Prynne that one of this man's shoulders rose higher than the other. Again, at the first instant of perceiving that thin visage, and the slight deformity of the figure, she pressed her infant to her bosom with so convulsive a force that the poor babe uttered another cry of pain. But the mother did not seem to hear it.

At his arrival in the market-place, and some time before she saw him, the stranger had bent his eyes on Hester Prynne. His face darkened with some powerful emotion, which, nevertheless, he so instantaneously controlled by an effort of his will. When he found the eyes of Hester Prynne fastened on his own, and saw that she appeared to recognize him, he slowly and calmly raised his finger, made a gesture with it in the air, and laid it on his lips.

Then touching the shoulder of a townsman who stood near to him, he addressed him in a formal and courteous manner: "I pray you, good Sir," said he, "who is this woman? and wherefore is she here set up to public shame?"

"You must needs be a stranger in this region, friend," answered the townsman, looking curiously at the questioner and his savage companion, "else you would surely have heard of Mistress Hester Prynne and her evil doings. She hath raised a great scandal, I promise you, in godly Master Dimmesdale's church."

"You say truly," replied the other; "I am a stranger, and have been a wanderer, sorely against my will. Will it please you, therefore, to tell me of Hester Prynne's, have I her name rightly? Of this woman's offences and what has brought her to yonder scaffold?"

"Yonder woman," said the townsman, "was the wife of a certain learned man, English by birth, but who had long ago dwelt in Amsterdam, whence some good time agone he was minded to cross over and cast in his lot with us of the Massachusetts. To this purpose he sent his wife before him, remaining himself to look after some necessary affairs. Marry, good Sir, in some two years, or less, that the woman has been a dweller here in Boston, no tidings have come of this learned gentleman, Master Prynne."

"Ah! I conceive you," said the stranger with a bitter smile. "And who, by your favor, Sir, may be the father of yonder babe, it is some three or four months old, I should judge, which Mistress Prynne is holding in her arms?"

"Of a truth, friend, that matter remains a riddle," answered the townsman. "Madame Hester absolutely refuses to speak, and the magistrates have laid their heads together in vain."

"The learned man," observed the stranger with another smile, "should come himself to look into the mystery."

"It behooves him well if he be still in life," responded the townsman. "Now, good Sir, our Massachusetts magistracy, they have not been bold to put in force the extremity of our righteous law against her. The penalty thereof is death. But in their great mercy and tenderness of heart they have doomed Mistress Prynne to stand only a space of three hours on the platform of the pillory, and then and thereafter, for the remainder of her natural life to wear a mark of shame upon her bosom."

He bowed courteously to the communicative townsman, and whispering a few words to his Indian attendant, they both made their way through the crowd.

While this passed, Hester Prynne had been standing on her pedestal, still with a fixed gaze towards the stranger; so fixed a gaze that, at moments of intense absorption, all other objects in the visible world seemed to vanish, leaving only him and her. Dreadful as it was, she was conscious of a shelter in the presence of these thousand witnesses. It was better to stand thus, with so many betwixt him and her, than to greet him face to face, they two alone. Involved in these thoughts, she scarcely heard a voice behind her until it had repeated her name more than once, in a loud and solemn tone, audible to the whole multitude.

"Hearken unto me, Hester Prynne!" said the voice.

It has already been noticed that directly over the platform on which Hester Prynne stood was a kind of balcony, or open gallery, appended to the meeting-house. Here, to witness the scene which we are describing, sat Governor Bellingham himself with four sergeants about his chair, bearing halberds, as a guard of honor. He wore a dark feather in his hat, a border of embroidery on his cloak, and a black velvet tunic. Hester Prynne now turned her face. She seemed conscious, indeed, that whatever sympathy she might expect lay in the larger and warmer heart of the multitude; for, as she lifted her eyes towards the balcony, the unhappy woman grew pale, and trembled.

The voice which had called her attention was that of the reverend and famous John Wilson, the eldest clergyman of Boston. There he stood, with a border of grizzled locks beneath his skull-cap, while his grey eyes, accustomed to the shaded light of his study, were winking, like those of Hester's infant, in the unadulterated sunshine.

"Hester Prynne," said the clergyman, "I have striven with my young brother here, under whose preaching of the Word you have been privileged to sit", here Mr. Wilson laid his hand on the shoulder of a pale young man beside him, "I have sought to persuade this godly youth, that he should deal with you. Knowing your natural temper better than I, he could the better judge what arguments to use, whether of tenderness or terror, such as might prevail over your hardness and obstinacy, insomuch that you should no longer hide the name of him who tempted you to this grievous fall. But he opposes to me that it were wronging the very nature of woman to force her to lay open her heart's secrets in such broad daylight. Truly, the shame lay in the commission of the sin. What say you to it, once again, brother Dimmesdale? Must it be thou, or I, that shall deal with this poor sinner's soul?"

There was a murmur among the dignified and reverend occupants of the balcony; and Governor Bellingham gave expression to its purport, speaking in an authoritative voice, although tempered with respect towards the youthful clergyman whom he addressed:

"Good Master Dimmesdale," said he, "the responsibility of this woman's soul lies greatly with you. It behooves you; therefore, to exhort her to repentance and to confession, as a proof and consequence thereof."

The directness of this appeal drew the eyes of the whole crowd upon the Reverend Mr. Dimmesdale. Notwithstanding his high native gifts and scholar-like attainments, there was an air about this young minister, an apprehensive, a startled, a half-frightened look, as of a being who felt himself quite astray, and at a loss in the pathway of human existence, and could only be at ease in some seclusion of his own. Therefore, so far as his duties would permit, he trod in the shadowy by-paths, and thus kept himself simple and childlike, coming forth, when occasion was, with a freshness, and fragrance, and dewy purity of thought, which, as many people said, affected them like the speech of an angel.

The Reverend Mr. Dimmesdale bent his head, in silent prayer, as it seemed, and then came forward.

"Hester Prynne," said he, leaning over the balcony and looking down steadfastly into her eyes, "thou hearest what this good man says, and seest the accountability under which I labor. If thou feelest it to be for thy soul's peace, and that thy earthly punishment will thereby be made more effectual to salvation, I charge thee to speak out the name of thy fellow-sinner and fellow-sufferer!"

The young pastor's voice was tremulously sweet, rich, deep, and broken. The feeling that it so evidently manifested, rather than the direct purport of the words, caused it to vibrate within all hearts, and brought the listeners into one accord of sympathy. Even the poor baby at Hester's bosom was affected by the same influence, for it directed its hitherto vacant gaze towards Mr. Dimmesdale, and held up its little arms with a half-pleased, half-plaintive murmur.

Hester shook her head.

"Woman, transgress not beyond the limits of Heaven's mercy!" cried the Reverend Mr. Wilson, more harshly than before. "Speak out the name! That, and thy repentance, may avail to take the scarlet letter off thy breast."

"Never," replied Hester Prynne, looking, not at Mr. Wilson, but into the deep and troubled eyes of the younger clergyman. "It is too deeply branded. Ye cannot take it off. And would that I might endure his agony as well as mine!"

"Speak, woman!" said another voice, coldly and sternly, proceeding from the crowd about the scaffold, "Speak; and give your child a father!"

"I will not speak!" answered Hester, turning pale as death, but responding to this voice, which she too surely recognized. "And my child must seek a heavenly father; she shall never know an earthly one!"

Discerning the impracticable state of the poor culprit's mind, the elder clergyman, who had carefully prepared himself for the occasion, addressed to the multitude a discourse on sin. So forcibly did he dwell upon this symbol that it assumed new terrors in their imagination, and seemed to derive its scarlet hue from the flames of the infernal pit. Hester Prynne, meanwhile, kept her place upon the pedestal of shame, with glazed eyes, and an air of weary indifference. The infant, during the latter portion of her ordeal, pierced the air with its wailings and screams; she strove to hush it mechanically, but seemed scarcely to sympathize with its trouble. With the same hard demeanor, she was led back to prison, and vanished from the public gaze within its iron-clamped portal. It was whispered by those who peered after her that the scarlet letter threw a lurid gleam along the dark passage-way of the interior.

CHAPTER 4: THE INTERVIEW

As night approached, Master Brackett, the jailer, thought fit to introduce a physician. To say the truth, there was much need of professional assistance, not merely for Hester herself, but still more urgently for the child, who, drawing its sustenance from the maternal bosom, seemed to have drank in with it all the turmoil, the anguish and despair, which pervaded the mother's system. It now writhed in convulsions of pain.

Closely following the jailer into the dismal apartment, appeared that individual, of singular aspect whose presence in the crowd had been of such deep interest to the wearer of the scarlet letter. He was lodged in the prison, not as suspected of any offence, but as the most convenient and suitable mode of disposing of him, until the magistrates should have conferred with the Indian sagamores respecting his ransom. His name was announced as Roger Chillingworth. The jailer, after ushering him into the room, remained a moment, marveling at the comparative quiet that followed his entrance; for Hester Prynne had immediately become as still as death, although the child continued to moan.

The stranger had entered the room with the characteristic quietude of the profession to which he announced himself as belonging. Nor did his demeanor change when the withdrawal of the prison keeper left him face to face with the woman. His first care was given to the child. He examined the infant carefully, and then proceeded to unclasp a leathern case, which he took from beneath his dress. It appeared to contain medical preparations, one of which he mingled with a cup of water.

"My old studies in alchemy," observed he, "and my sojourn among a people well versed in the kindly properties of simples, have made a better physician of me than many that claim the medical degree. Here, woman! The child is yours. Administer this draught, therefore, with thine own hand."

Hester repelled the offered medicine, at the same time gazing with strongly marked apprehension into his face. "Wouldst thou avenge thyself on the innocent babe?" whispered she.

"Foolish woman!" responded the physician, half coldly, half soothingly. "What should ail me to harm this misbegotten and miserable babe?"

As she still hesitated, being, in fact, in no reasonable state of mind, he took the infant in his arms, and himself administered the draught. It soon proved its efficacy. The moans of the little patient subsided and in a few moments it sank into a profound and dewy slumber. The physician next bestowed his attention on the mother. With calm and intent scrutiny, he felt her pulse, looked into her eyes—a gaze that made her heart shrink and shudder, because so familiar, and yet so strange and cold—and, finally, satisfied with his investigation, proceeded to mingle another draught.

"I have learned many new secrets in the wilderness," remarked he, "and here is one of them. Drink it! It may be less soothing than a sinless conscience. That I cannot give thee."

He presented the cup to Hester, who received it with a slow, earnest look into his face; not precisely a look of fear, yet full of doubt and questioning as to what his purposes might be. She looked also at her slumbering child.

"I have thought of death," said she, "have wished for it, would even have prayed for it, were it fit that such as I should pray for anything. Yet, if death be in this cup, I bid thee think again, ere thou beholdest me quaff it. See! it is even now at my lips."

"Drink, then," replied he, still with the same cold composure. "Dost thou know me so little, Hester Prynne? Even if I imagine a scheme of vengeance, what could I do better for my object than to let thee live so that this burning shame may still blaze upon thy bosom?" As he spoke, he laid his long fore-finger on the scarlet letter, which forthwith seemed to scorch into Hester's breast, as if it had been red hot. He noticed her involuntary gesture, and smiled. "Live, therefore, and bear about thy doom with thee, in the eyes of men and women, in the eyes of him whom you called a husband, and in the eyes of your child!"

Without further expostulation or delay, Hester Prynne drained the cup, and, at the motion of the man of skill, seated herself on the bed, where the child was sleeping; while he drew the only chair which the room afforded, and took his own seat beside her. She could not but tremble at these preparations; for she felt that he was next to treat with her as the man whom she had most deeply and irreparably injured.

"Hester," said he, "I ask not wherefore, nor how thou hast fallen into the pit. The reason is not far to seek. It was my folly, and thy weakness. I, a man of thought, a man already in decay, having given my best years to feed the hungry dream of knowledge, what had I to do with youth and beauty like thine own? Misshapen from my birth-hour, how could I delude myself with the idea that intellectual gifts might veil physical deformity in a young girl's fantasy? Men call me wise. If sages were ever wise in their own behoove, I might have foreseen all this. From the moment when we came down the old church-steps together, a married pair, I might have beheld the bale-fire of that scarlet letter blazing at the end of our path!"

"Thou knowest," said Hester, "thou knowest that I was frank with thee. I felt no love, nor feigned any."

"True," replied he. "It was my folly! I have said it. But, up to that epoch of my life, I had lived in vain. The world had been so cheerless! My heart was a habitation large enough for many guests, but lonely and chill, and without a household fire. And so, Hester, I drew thee into my heart, into its innermost chamber, and sought to warm thee by the warmth which thy presence made there!"

"I have greatly wronged thee," murmured Hester.

"We have wronged each other," answered he. "Mine was the first wrong, when I betrayed thy budding youth into a false and unnatural relation with my decay. I seek no vengeance, plot no evil against thee. But, Hester, the man lives who has wronged us both! Who is he?"

"Ask me not!" replied Hester Prynne, looking firmly into his face. "That thou shalt never know!"

"Never, sayest thou?" rejoined he, with a smile of dark and self-relying intelligence. "Never know him! Believe me, Hester, there are few things hidden from the man who devotes himself earnestly and unreservedly to the solution of a mystery. Thou mayest cover up thy secret from the prying multitude. But, as for me, I come to the inquest with other senses than they possess. I shall seek this man. There is a sympathy that will make me conscious of him. I shall see him tremble. I shall feel myself shudder, suddenly and unawares. Sooner or later, he must needs be mine."

The eyes of the wrinkled scholar glowed so intensely upon her, that Hester Prynne clasped her hand over her heart, dreading lest he should read the secret there at once.

"Thou wilt not reveal his name? Not the less he is mine," resumed he, with a look of confidence, as if destiny were at one with him. "He bears no letter of infamy wrought into his garment, but I shall read it on his heart. Yet fear not for him! Think not that I shall interfere with Heaven's own method of retribution, or, to my own loss, betray him to the gripe of human law. Neither do thou imagine that I shall contrive aught against his life."

"Thy acts are like mercy," said Hester, bewildered and appalled; "but thy words interpret thee as a terror!"

"One thing, thou that wast my wife, I would enjoin upon thee," continued the scholar. "Thou hast kept the secret of thy paramour. Keep, likewise, mine! There are none in this land that know me. Breathe not to any human soul that thou didst ever call me husband! Here, on this wild outskirt of the earth, I shall pitch my tent. Thou and thine, Hester Prynne, belong to me. My home is where thou art and where he is. But betray me not!"

"Wherefore dost thou desire it?" inquired Hester, shrinking, she hardly knew why, from this secret bond. "Why not announce thyself openly, and cast me off at once?"

"It may be," he replied, "because I will not encounter the dishonor that besmirches the husband of a faithless woman. It may be for other reasons. Enough, it is my purpose to live and die unknown. If you fail me in this, beware! His fame, his position, his life will be in my hands. Beware!"

"I will keep thy secret, as I have his," said Hester.

"Swear it!" rejoined he.

And she took the oath.

"And now, Mistress Prynne," said old Roger Chillingworth, as he was hereafter to be named, "I leave thee alone: alone with thy infant and the scarlet letter!"

"Why dost thou smile so at me?" inquired Hester, troubled at the expression of his eyes. "Have you enticed me into a bond that will prove the ruin of my soul?"

"Not your soul," he answered, with another smile. "No, not yours!"

CHAPTER 5: HESTER AT HER NEEDLE

Hester Prynne's term of confinement was now at an end. Her prison-door was thrown open, and she came forth into the sunshine. Perhaps there was a more real torture in her first unattended footsteps from the threshold of the prison than even in the procession and spectacle that have been described at which all mankind was summoned to point its finger. Then, she was supported by an unnatural tension of the nerves, and by all the combative energy of her character. It was, moreover, a separate and insulated event, to occur but once in her lifetime. But now, with this unattended walk from her prison door, began the daily custom; and she must either sustain and carry it forward by the ordinary resources of her nature, or sink beneath it. Tomorrow would bring its own trial with it; so would the next day, and so would the next. Throughout them all, giving up her individuality, she would become the general symbol at which the preacher and moralist might point, and in which they might vivify and embody their images of woman's frailty and sinful passion. Thus the young and pure would be taught to look at her, with the scarlet letter flaming on her breast. And over her grave, the infamy that she must carry thither would be her only monument.

It may seem marvelous that, with the world before her, kept by no restrictive clause of her condemnation within the limits of the Puritan settlement, that this woman should still call that place her home, where, and where only, she must needs be the type of shame. But there is a fatality, a feeling so irresistible and inevitable that it has the force of doom, which almost invariably compels human beings to linger around and haunt, ghost-like, the spot where some great and marked event has given the color to their lifetime; and, still the more irresistibly, the darker the tinge that saddens it. Her sin, her ignominy, were the roots which she had struck into the soil. All other scenes of earth were foreign to her in comparison. The chain that bound her here was of iron links, and galling to her inmost soul, but could never be broken.

It might be that another feeling kept her within the scene and pathway that had been so fatal. There dwelt one with whom she deemed herself connected in a union that, unrecognized on earth, would bring them together before the bar of final judgment. What she compelled herself to believe, what, finally, she reasoned upon as her motive for continuing a resident of New England, was half a truth, and half a self-delusion. Here, she said to herself had been the scene of her guilt, and here should be the scene of her earthly punishment; and so, perchance, the torture of her daily shame would at length purge her soul.

Hester Prynne, therefore, did not flee. On the outskirts of the town there was a small thatched cottage. It had been built by an earlier settler, and abandoned, because the soil about it was too sterile for cultivation. It stood on the shore, looking across a basin of the sea at the forest-covered hills, towards the west. A clump of scrubby trees did not so much conceal the cottage from view as seem to denote that here was some object which would fain have been, or at least ought to be, concealed. In this little lonesome dwelling Hester established herself, with her infant child. A mystic shadow of suspicion immediately attached itself to the spot. Children would creep nigh enough to behold her plying her needle at the cottage-window, or standing in the doorway, or laboring in her little garden, or coming forth along the pathway that led townward, and, discerning the scarlet letter on her breast, would scamper off with a strange contagious fear.

Lonely as was Hester's situation, and without a friend on earth who dared to show himself, she, however, incurred no risk of want. She possessed an art that sufficed to supply food for her thriving infant and herself. It was the art of needle-work. She bore on her breast, in the curiously embroidered letter, a specimen of her delicate and imaginative skill. Here, indeed, in the sable simplicity that generally characterized the Puritanical modes of dress, there might be an infrequent call for the finer productions of her handiwork. Yet the taste of the age, demanding whatever was elaborate in compositions of this kind, did not fail to extend its influence over our stern progenitors. Public ceremonies, such as ordinations, the installation of magistrates, and all that could give majesty to the forms in which a new government manifested itself to the people, were, as a matter of policy, marked by a stately and well-conducted ceremonial, and a somber, but yet a studied magnificence. Deep ruffs, painfully wrought bands, and gorgeously embroidered gloves, were all deemed necessary to the official state of men assuming the reins of power. There was a frequent and characteristic demand for such labor as Hester Prynne could supply. Baby-linen afforded still another possibility of toil and emolument.

By degrees her handiwork became what would now be termed the fashion. Her needle-work was seen on the ruff of the Governor; military men wore it on their scarfs, and the minister on his band; it decked the baby's little cap; it was shut up, to be mildewed and molder away, in the coffins of the dead. But it is not recorded that, in a single instance, her skill was called in to embroider the white veil which was to cover the pure blushes of a bride. The exception indicated the ever relentless vigor with which society frowned upon her sin.

Hester sought not to acquire anything beyond a subsistence, of the plainest and most ascetic description, for herself, and a simple abundance for her child. Her own dress was of the coarsest materials and the most somber hue, with only that one ornament, the scarlet letter, which it was her doom to wear. The child's attire, on the other hand, was distinguished by a fantastic ingenuity, which served, indeed, to heighten the airy charm that early began to develop itself in the little girl, but which appeared to have also a deeper meaning. We may speak further of it hereafter. Except for that small expenditure in the decoration of her infant, Hester bestowed all her superfluous means in charity, on wretches less miserable than herself, and who not infrequently insulted the hand that fed them. It is probable that there was an idea of penance in devoting so many hours to such rude handiwork. She had in her nature a rich, voluptuous, Oriental characteristic, which, save in the exquisite productions of her needle, found nothing else to exercise itself upon. Like all other joys, she rejected it as sin.

In this manner, Hester Prynne came to have a part to perform in the world. In all her intercourse with society, however, there was nothing that made her feel as if she belonged to it. Every gesture, every word, and even the silence of those with whom she came in contact, implied that she was banished. It was not an age of delicacy; and her position, although she understood it well, and was in little danger of forgetting it, was often brought before her vivid self-perception, like a new anguish, by the rudest touch upon the tenderest spot. The poor, as we have already said, often reviled the hand that was stretched forth to succor them. Dames of elevated rank, likewise, whose doors she entered in the way of her occupation, were accustomed to distil drops of bitterness into her heart. Hester had schooled herself long and well; and she never responded to these attacks, save by a flush of crimson that rose irrepressibly over her pale cheek. She was patient, a martyr, indeed but she fore bore to pray for enemies, lest, in spite of her forgiving aspirations, the words of the blessing should stubbornly twist themselves into a curse.

Continually, and in a thousand other ways, did she feel the innumerable throbs of anguish that had been so cunningly contrived for her by the undying, the ever-active sentence of the Puritan tribunal. Clergymen paused in the streets, to address words of exhortation, that brought a crowd, around the poor, sinful woman. If she entered a church, trusting to share the Sabbath smile of the Universal Father, it was often her mishap to find herself the text of the discourse. She grew to have a dread of children; for they had imbibed from their parents a vague idea of something horrible in this dreary woman gliding silently through the town, with never any companion but one only child. Therefore, first allowing her to pass, they pursued her at a distance with shrill cries, and the utterances of a word that had no distinct purport to their own minds, but was none the less terrible to her. From first to last, in short, Hester Prynne had always this dreadful agony in feeling a human eye upon the token; the spot never grew callous; it seemed, on the contrary, to grow more sensitive with daily torture.

But sometimes, she felt an eye, a human eye, upon the ignominious brand, that seemed to give a momentary relief, as if half of her agony were shared. Had Hester sinned alone?

Her imagination was somewhat affected, and, had she been of a softer moral and intellectual fiber would have been still more so, by the strange and solitary anguish of her life. Walking to and fro, with those lonely footsteps it now and then appeared to Hester that the scarlet letter had endowed her with a new sense. She shuddered to believe that it gave her a sympathetic knowledge of the hidden sin in other hearts. She was terror-stricken by the revelations that were thus made. That the outward guise of purity was but a lie, and that, if truth were everywhere to be shown, a scarlet letter would blaze forth on many a bosom besides Hester Prynne's? Such loss of faith is ever one of the saddest results of sin. Be it accepted as a proof that all was not corrupt in this poor victim of her own frailty, and man's hard law, that Hester Prynne yet struggled to believe that no fellow-mortal was guilty like herself.

The vulgar, had a story about the scarlet letter which we might readily work up into a terrific legend. They averred that the symbol was not mere scarlet cloth but was red-hot with infernal fire and could be seen glowing all alight whenever Hester Prynne walked abroad in the night-time. And we must needs say it seared Hester's bosom so deeply, that perhaps there was more truth in the rumor than our modern incredulity may be inclined to admit.

CHAPTER 6: PEARL

We have as yet hardly spoken of the infant. She named the infant "Pearl," as being of great price, purchased with all she had, her mother's only treasure! Man had marked this woman's sin by a scarlet letter. God, as a direct consequence of the sin which man thus punished, had given her a lovely child, whose place was on that same dishonored bosom, to connect her parent for ever with the race and descent of mortals, and to be finally a blessed soul in heaven! Yet these thoughts affected Hester Prynne less with hope than apprehension. Day after day she looked fearfully into the child's expanding nature, ever dreading to detect some dark and wild peculiarity that should correspond with the guiltiness to which she owed her being.

Certainly there was no physical defect. By its perfect shape the infant was worthy to have been brought forth in Eden. The child was not clad in rustic weeds. Her mother had bought the richest tissues that could be procured, and allowed her imaginative faculty its full play in the arrangement and decoration of the dresses which the child wore before the public eye. There was an absolute circle of radiance around her. And yet a russet gown, torn and soiled with the child's rude play, made a picture of her just as perfect. Pearl's aspect was imbued with a spell of infinite variety; in this one child there were many children, comprehending the full scope between the wild-flower prettiness of a peasant-baby, and the pomp, in little, of an infant princess.

Her nature appeared to possess depth, too, as well as variety. The child could not be made amenable to rules. In giving her existence a great law had been broken; and the result was a being whose elements were perhaps beautiful and brilliant, but all in disorder. Hester could only account for the child's character by recalling what she herself had been during that momentous period while Pearl was imbibing her soul from the spiritual world. The mother's impassioned state had been the medium through which were transmitted to the unborn infant the rays of its moral life; and, however white and clear originally, they had taken the deep stains of crimson and gold, the fiery luster, the black shadow, and the untempered light of the intervening substance.

The discipline of the family in those days was of a far more rigid kind than now. Hester Prynne, nevertheless, the loving mother of this one child, ran little risk of erring on the side of undue severity. She early sought to impose a tender but strict control over the infant immortality that was committed to her charge. But the task was beyond her skill. Hester was ultimately compelled to stand aside and permit the child to be swayed by her own impulses. Her only real comfort was when the child lay in the placidity of sleep. Then she was sure of her, and tasted hours of quiet, sad, delicious happiness; until, perhaps with that perverse expression glimmering from beneath her opening lids, little Pearl awoke!

How soon did Pearl arrive at an age that was capable of social intercourse! And then what a happiness would it have been could Hester Prynne have heard her clear, bird-like voice mingling with the uproar of other childish voices, and have distinguished and unraveled her own darling's tones. But this could never be. Pearl was a born outcast of the infantile world. Nothing was more remarkable than the instinct, as it seemed, with which the child comprehended her loneliness. Never since her release from prison had Hester met the public gaze without her. Pearl saw, and gazed intently, but never sought to make acquaintance. If the children gathered about her, as they sometimes did, Pearl would grow positively terrible in her puny wrath, snatching up stones to fling at them, with shrill, incoherent exclamations, that made her mother tremble, because they had so much the sound of a witch's anathemas in some unknown tongue.

These outbreaks of a fierce temper had a kind of value, and even comfort for the mother; because there was at least an intelligible earnestness in the mood. It appalled her, nevertheless, to discern here, again, a shadowy reflection of the evil that had existed in herself. Mother and daughter stood together in the same circle of seclusion from human society; and in the nature of the child seemed to be perpetuated those unquiet elements that had distracted Hester Prynne before Pearl's birth, but had since begun to be soothed away by the softening influences of maternity.

One peculiarity of the child's deportment remains yet to be told. The very first thing which she had noticed in her life, was the scarlet letter on Hester's bosom! One day, as her mother stooped over the cradle, the infant's eyes had been caught by the glimmering of the gold embroidery about the letter; and putting up her little hand she grasped at it, smiling, not doubtfully, but with a decided gleam, that gave her face the look of a much older child. From that epoch, except when the child was asleep, Hester had never felt a moment's safety: not a moment's calm enjoyment of her. Weeks, it is true, would sometimes elapse, during which Pearl's gaze might never once be fixed upon the scarlet letter; but then, again, it would come at unawares, like the stroke of sudden death, and always with that peculiar smile and odd expression of the eyes.

Once this freakish, elvish cast came into the child's eyes while Hester was looking at her own image in them. She fancied that she beheld, not her own miniature portrait, but another face in the small black mirror of Pearl's eye. It was a face, fiend-like, full of smiling malice, yet bearing the semblance of features that she had known full well, though seldom with a smile, and never with malice in them. It was as if an evil spirit possessed the child, and had just then peeped forth in mockery. Many a time afterwards had Hester been tortured, though less vividly, by the same illusion.

In the afternoon of a certain summer's day, after Pearl grew big enough to run about, she amused herself with gathering handfuls of wild flowers, and flinging them, one by one, at her mother's bosom; dancing up and down like a little elf whenever she hit the scarlet letter. Hester's first motion had been to cover her bosom with her clasped hands. But whether from pride or resignation, or a feeling that her penance might best be wrought out by this unutterable pain, she resisted the impulse, and sat erect, pale as death, looking sadly into little Pearl's wild eyes. At last, her shot being all expended, the child stood still and gazed at Hester, with that little laughing image of a fiend peeping out or, whether it peeped or no, her mother so imagined it, from the unsearchable abyss of her black eyes.

"Child, what art thou?" cried the mother.

"Oh, I am your little Pearl!" answered the child.

"Thou art not my child! Thou art no Pearl of mine!" said the mother half playfully; for it was often the case that a sportive impulse came over her in the midst of her deepest suffering. "Tell me, then, what thou art, and who sent thee hither?"

"Tell me, mother!" said the child, seriously, coming up to Hester, and pressing herself close to her knees. "Do thou tell me!"

"Thy Heavenly Father sent thee!" answered Hester Prynne.

"He did not send me!" cried she, positively. "I have no Heavenly Father!"

"Hush, Pearl, hush! Thou must not talk so!" answered the mother, suppressing a groan. "He sent us all into the world. He sent even me, thy mother."

But Hester could not resolve the query. She remembered the talk of the neighboring townspeople who said that poor little Pearl was a demon offspring.

CHAPTER 7: THE GOVERNOR'S HALL

Hester Prynne went one day to the mansion of Governor Bellingham, with a pair of gloves which she had fringed and embroidered to his order, and which were to be worn on some great occasion of state.

Another and far more important reason than the delivery of a pair of embroidered gloves, impelled Hester, at this time, to seek an interview with a personage of so much power and activity in the affairs of the settlement. It had reached her ears that there was a design on the part of some of the leading inhabitants to deprive her of her child. On the supposition that Pearl, as already hinted, was of demon origin, these good people not unreasonably argued that a Christian interest in the mother's soul required them to remove such a stumbling-block from her path. If the child, on the other hand, were really capable of moral and religious growth, then, surely, it would enjoy all the fairer prospect of these advantages by being transferred to wiser and better guardianship than Hester Prynne's. Among those who promoted the design, Governor Bellingham was said to be one of the most busy.

Full of concern Hester Prynne set forth from her solitary cottage. Little Pearl, of course, was her companion. She was now of an age to run lightly along by her mother's side. We have spoken of Pearl's rich and luxuriant beauty. There was fire in her and throughout her: she seemed the unpremeditated offshoot of a passionate moment. Her mother, in contriving the child's garb, had allowed the gorgeous tendencies of her imagination their full play, arraying her in a crimson velvet tunic of a peculiar cut, abundantly embroidered in fantasies and flourishes of gold thread.

But it was a remarkable attribute of this garb, and indeed, of the child's whole appearance, that it irresistibly and inevitably reminded the beholder of the token which Hester Prynne was doomed to wear upon her bosom. It was the scarlet letter in another form: the scarlet letter endowed with life!

As the two wayfarers came within the precincts of the town, the children of the Puritans looked up from their play and spoke gravely one to another: "Behold, verily, there is the woman of the scarlet letter: and of a truth, moreover, there is the likeness of the scarlet letter running along by her side! Come, therefore, and let us fling mud at them!"

But Pearl, who was a dauntless child, suddenly made a rush at the knot of her enemies, and put them all to flight. The victory accomplished, Pearl returned quietly to her mother, and looked up, smiling, into her face.

Without further adventure, they reached the dwelling of Governor Bellingham. It had a very cheery aspect; the walls being overspread with a kind of stucco, in which fragments of broken glass were plentifully intermixed; so that, when the sunshine fell aslant-wise over the front of the edifice, it glittered and sparkled as if diamonds had been flung against it by the double handful.

They approached the door. Lifting the iron hammer that hung at the portal, Hester Prynne gave a summons, which was answered by one of the Governor's bond servants.

"Is the worshipful Governor Bellingham within?" inquired Hester.

"Yea, forsooth," replied the bond-servant, staring with wide-open eyes at the scarlet letter, which, being a new-comer in the country, he had never before seen. "Yea, his honorable worship is within. But he hath a godly minister or two with him, and likewise a leech. Ye may not see his worship now."

"Nevertheless, I will enter," answered Hester Prynne; and the bond-servant, perhaps judging from the decision of her air, and the glittering symbol in her bosom, that she was a great lady in the land, offered no opposition.

On the wall hung a row of portraits, representing the forefathers of the Bellingham lineage, some with armor on their breasts, and others with stately ruffs and robes of peace. All were characterized by the sternness and severity which old portraits so invariably put on, as if they were the ghosts, rather than the pictures, of departed worthies, and were gazing with harsh and intolerant criticism at the pursuits and enjoyments of living men.

At about the center of the hall was suspended a suit of armor. It had been manufactured by a skillful armorer in London, the same year in which Governor Bellingham came over to New England. The helmet and breastplate were so highly burnished that they were aglow with white radiance, scattering an illumination everywhere about upon the floor.

Little Pearl, who was as greatly pleased with the gleaming armor as she had been with the glittering frontispiece of the house, spent some time looking into the polished mirror of the breastplate.

"Mother," cried she, "I see you here. Look! Look!"

Hester looked by way of humoring the child; and she saw that, owing to the peculiar effect of this convex mirror, the scarlet letter was represented in exaggerated and gigantic proportions, so as to be greatly the most prominent feature of her appearance. In truth, she seemed absolutely hidden behind it.

"Come along, Pearl," said she, drawing her away, "Come and look into this fair garden. It may be we shall see flowers there; more beautiful ones than we find in the woods."

Pearl ran to the bow-window and looked along the vista of a garden walk, carpeted with closely-shaven grass, and bordered with some rude and immature attempt at shrubbery. There were a few rose-bushes and a number of apple-trees. Pearl, seeing the rose-bushes, began to cry for a red rose, and would not be pacified.

"Hush, child, hush!" said her mother, earnestly. "Do not cry, dear little Pearl! I hear voices in the garden. The Governor is coming, and gentlemen along with him."

In fact, a number of persons were seen approaching towards the house. Pearl, in utter scorn of her mother's attempt to quiet her, gave an eldritch scream, and then became silent, not from any notion of obedience, but because the quick and mobile curiosity of her disposition was excited by the appearance of those new personages.

CHAPTER 8: THE ELF-CHILD AND THE MINISTER

Governor Bellingham, in a loose gown and easy cap walked foremost, and appeared to be showing off his estate. The impression made by his aspect, so rigid and severe, and frost-bitten with more than autumnal age, was hardly in keeping with the appliances of worldly enjoyment wherewith he had evidently done his utmost to surround himself. But it is an error to suppose that our great forefathers, though accustomed to speak and think of human existence as a state merely of trial and warfare, made it a matter of conscience to reject such means of comfort, or even luxury. The venerable pastor, John Wilson, was seen over Governor Bellingham's shoulder. The old clergyman had a long established and legitimate taste for all good and comfortable things, and however stern he might show himself in the pulpit, or in his public reproof of such transgressions as that of Hester Prynne, still, the genial benevolence of his private life had won him warmer affection than was accorded to any of his professional contemporaries.

Behind the Governor and Mr. Wilson came two other guests: one, the Reverend Arthur Dimmesdale, whom the reader may remember as having taken a brief and reluctant part in the scene of Hester Prynne's disgrace; and, in close companionship with him, old Roger Chillingworth, a person of great skill in physic, who for two or three years past had been settled in the town. It was understood that this learned man was the physician as well as friend of the young minister, whose health had severely suffered of late by his too unreserved self-sacrifice to the labors and duties of the pastoral relation.

The Governor, in advance of his visitors, ascended one or two steps, and, throwing open the leaves of the great hall window, found himself close to little Pearl. The shadow of the curtain fell on Hester Prynne, and partially concealed her.

"What have we here?" said Governor Bellingham, looking with surprise at the scarlet little figure before him. But how gat such a guest into my hall?"

"Ay, indeed!" cried good old Mr. Wilson. "What little bird of scarlet plumage may this be?"

"I am mother's child," answered the scarlet vision, "and my name is Pearl!"

"Pearl?" responded the old minister, putting forth his hand in a vain attempt to pat little Pearl on the cheek. "But where is this mother of thine? Ah! I see," he added; and, turning to Governor Bellingham, whispered, "This is the selfsame child of whom we have held speech together; and behold here the unhappy woman, Hester Prynne, her mother!"

Governor Bellingham stepped through the window into the hall, followed by his three guests.

"Hester Prynne," said he, fixing his naturally stern regard on the wearer of the scarlet letter, "there hath been much question concerning thee of late. Speak thou, the child's own mother! Were it not, thinkest thou, for thy little one's temporal and eternal welfare that she be taken out of thy charge, and clad soberly, and disciplined strictly, and instructed in the truths of heaven and earth? What canst thou do for the child in this kind?"

"I can teach my little Pearl what I have learned from this!" answered Hester Prynne, laying her finger on the red token.

"Good Master Wilson," said Bellingham, "I pray you, examine this Pearl, since that is her name, and see whether she hath had such Christian nurture as befits a child of her age."

The old minister seated himself in an arm-chair and made an effort to draw Pearl betwixt his knees. But the child, unaccustomed to the touch or familiarity of any but her mother, escaped through the open window, and stood on the upper step, looking like a wild tropical bird of rich plumage, ready to take flight into the upper air.

"Pearl," said he, with great solemnity, "thou must take heed to instruction, that so, in due season, thou mayest wear in thy bosom the pearl of great price. Canst thou tell me, my child, who made thee?"

After putting her finger in her mouth, with many ungracious refusals to answer good Mr. Wilson's question, the child finally announced that she had not been made at all, but had been plucked by her mother off the bush of wild roses that grew by the prison-door.

Old Roger Chillingworth, with a smile on his face, whispered something in the young clergyman's ear. Hester Prynne looked at the man of skill, and even then, with her fate hanging in the balance, was startled to perceive what a change had come over his features, how much uglier they were, since the days when she had familiarly known him.

"This is awful!" cried the Governor, slowly recovering from the astonishment into which Pearl's response had thrown him. "Here is a child of three years old, and she cannot tell who made her! Without question, she is equally in the dark as to her soul, its present depravity, and future destiny!"

Hester caught hold of Pearl, and drew her forcibly into her arms. Alone in the world, cast off by it, and with this sole treasure to keep her heart alive, she felt that she possessed indefeasible rights against the world, and was ready to defend them to the death.

"God gave me the child!" cried she. "She is my happiness and she is my torture, none the less! Pearl keeps me here in life! Ye shall not take her! I will die first!"

"My poor woman," said the not unkind old minister, "the child shall be well cared for—far better than thou canst do for it."

"God gave her into my keeping!" repeated Hester Prynne, raising her voice almost to a shriek. "I will not give her up!" And here by a sudden impulse, she turned to the young clergyman, Mr. Dimmesdale, at whom, up to this moment, she had seemed hardly so much as once to direct her eyes. "Speak thou for me!" cried she. "Thou wast my pastor, and hadst charge of my soul, and knowest me better than these men can. I will not lose the child! Thou knowest for thou hast sympathies which these men lack. Thou knowest what is in my heart and what are a mother's rights!"

The young minister at once came forward, pale, and holding his hand over his heart. His large dark eyes had a world of pain in their troubled and melancholy depth.

"There is truth in what she says," began the minister, with a voice sweet, tremulous, but powerful, insomuch that the hall re-echoed and the hollow armor rang with it, "God gave her the child, and gave her, too, an instinctive knowledge of its nature and requirements."

"It must be even so," resumed the minister. "This child of its father's guilt and its mother's shame has come from the hand of God, to work in many ways upon her heart, who pleads so earnestly and with such bitterness of spirit the right to keep her. It was meant for a blessing—for the one blessing of her life! It was meant, doubtless, the mother herself hath told us, for a retribution, too. Hath she not expressed this thought in the garb of the poor child, so forcibly reminding us of that red symbol which sears her bosom?"

"She recognizes," continued Mr. Dimmesdale. "The solemn miracle which God hath wrought in the existence of that child. Therefore it is good for this poor, sinful woman, that she hath an infant immortality, a being to be trained up by her to righteousness. For Hester Prynne's sake, then, and no less for the poor child's sake, let us leave them as Providence hath seen fit to place them!"

"You speak, my friend, with a strange earnestness," said old Roger Chillingworth, smiling at him.

"And there is a weighty import in what my young brother hath spoken," added the Rev. Mr. Wilson. "What say you, worshipful Master Bellingham? Hath he not pleaded well for the poor woman?"

"Indeed hath he," answered the magistrate; "and hath adduced such arguments, that we will even leave the matter as it now stands; so long, at least, as there shall be no further scandal in the woman."

The young minister, on ceasing to speak had withdrawn a few steps from the group, and stood with his face partially concealed in the heavy folds of the window-curtain. Pearl, that wild and flighty little elf stole softly towards him, and taking his hand in the grasp of both her own, laid her cheek against it; a caress so tender, and withal so unobtrusive, that her mother, who was looking on, asked herself, "Is that my Pearl?" The minister looked round, laid his hand on the child's head, hesitated an instant, and then kissed her brow. Little Pearl's unwonted mood of sentiment lasted no longer; she laughed, and went capering down the hall so airily, that old Mr. Wilson raised a question whether even her tiptoes touched the floor.

The affair being so satisfactorily concluded, Hester Prynne, with Pearl, departed from the house. As they descended the steps, it is averred that the lattice of a chamber-window was thrown open, and forth into the sunny day was thrust the face of Mistress Hibbins, Governor Bellingham's bitter-tempered sister, and the same who, a few years later, was executed as a witch.

"Hist, hist!" said she, while her ill-omened physiognomy seemed to cast a shadow over the cheerful newness of the house. "Wilt thou go with us to-night? There will be a merry company in the forest; and I well-nigh promised the Black Man that comely Hester Prynne should make one."

"Make my excuse to him, so please you!" answered Hester, with a triumphant smile. "I must tarry at home, and keep watch over my little Pearl. Had they taken her from me, I would willingly have gone with thee into the forest, and signed my name in the Black Man's book too, and that with mine own blood!"

"We shall have thee there anon!" said the witch-lady, frowning, as she drew back her head.

But here was already an illustration of the young minister's argument against sundering the relation of a fallen mother to the offspring of her frailty. Even thus early had the child saved her from Satan's snare.

CHAPTER 9: THE LEECH

Under the appellation of Roger Chillingworth, the reader will remember, was hidden another name, which its former wearer had resolved should never more be spoken. Hester Prynne's matronly fame was trodden under all men's feet. Infamy was babbling around her in the public market-place. For the companions of her unspotted life, there remained nothing but the contagion of her dishonor; which would not fail to be distributed in strict accordance and proportion with the intimacy and sacredness of their previous relationship. Then why, since the choice was with himself, should the individual, whose connection with the fallen woman had been the most intimate and sacred of them all, come forward to vindicate his claim to an inheritance so little desirable?

In pursuance of this resolve, he took up his residence in the Puritan town as Roger Chillingworth, without other introduction than the learning and intelligence of which he possessed more than a common measure. As his studies, at a previous period of his life, had made him extensively acquainted with the medical science of the day, it was as a physician that he presented himself and as such was cordially received. Skilful men, of the medical and chirurgical profession, were of rare occurrence in the colony.

This learned stranger was exemplary as regarded at least the outward forms of a religious life; and early after his arrival, had chosen for his spiritual guide the Reverend Mr. Dimmesdale. The young divine, whose scholar-like renown still lived in Oxford, was considered by his more fervent admirers as little less than a heavenly ordained apostle. About this period, however, the health of Mr. Dimmesdale had evidently begun to fail. By those best acquainted with his habits, the paleness of the young minister's cheek was accounted for by his too earnest devotion to study, his scrupulous fulfillment of parochial duty. Some declared, Mr. Dimmesdale's form grew emaciated; his voice, though still rich and sweet, had a certain melancholy prophecy of decay in it; he was often observed, on any slight alarm or other sudden accident, to put his hand over his heart with first a flush and then a paleness, indicative of pain.

Such was the young clergyman's condition, and so imminent the prospect that his dawning light would be extinguished, all untimely, when Roger Chillingworth made his advent to the town. His first entry on the scene, few people could tell whence, dropping down as it were out of the sky or starting from the nether earth, had an aspect of mystery, which was easily heightened to the miraculous. He was now known to be a man of skill. Why, with such rank in the learned world, had he come hither? In answer to this query, a rumor gained ground that Heaven had wrought an absolute miracle by transporting an eminent Doctor of Physic from a German university bodily through the air and setting him down at the door of Mr. Dimmesdale's study!

This idea was countenanced by the strong interest which the physician ever manifested in the young clergyman; he attached himself to him as a parishioner. He expressed great alarm at his pastor's state of health, but was anxious to attempt the cure.

In this manner, the mysterious old Roger Chillingworth became the medical adviser of the Reverend Mr. Dimmesdale. As not only the disease interested the physician, but he was strongly moved to look into the character and qualities of the patient, these two men, so different in age, came gradually to spend much time together. For the sake of the minister's health, and to enable the leech to gather plants with healing balm in them, they took long walks on the sea-shore, or in the forest; mingling various walks with the splash and murmur of the waves, and the solemn wind-anthem among the tree-tops. There was a fascination for the minister in the company of the man of science. In truth, he was startled, if not shocked, to find this attribute in the physician. Mr. Dimmesdale was a true priest, a true religionist. In no state of society would he have been what is called a man of liberal views. Not the less, however, though with a tremulous enjoyment, did he feel the occasional relief of looking at the universe through the medium of another kind of intellect than those with which he habitually held converse.

Thus Roger Chillingworth scrutinized his patient carefully. He deemed it essential, it would seem, to know the man, before attempting to do him good. Wherever there is a heart and an intellect, the diseases of the physical frame are tinged with the peculiarities of these. So Roger Chillingworth, the man of skill, the kind and friendly physician, strove to go deep into his patient's bosom, delving among his principles, prying into his recollections, and probing everything with a cautious touch, like a treasure-seeker in a dark cavern. Few secrets can escape an investigator, who has opportunity and license to undertake such a quest, and skill to follow it up. A man burdened with a secret should especially avoid the intimacy of his physician.

A kind of intimacy grew up between these two cultivated minds, which had as wide a field as the whole sphere of human thought and study to meet upon and yet no secret, such as the physician fancied must exist there, ever stole out of the minister's consciousness into his companion's ear. The latter had his suspicions, indeed, that even the nature of Mr. Dimmesdale's bodily disease had never fairly been revealed to him.

After a time, at a hint from Roger Chillingworth, the friends of Mr. Dimmesdale effected an arrangement by which the two were lodged in the same house; so that every ebb and flow of the minister's life-tide might pass under the eye of his anxious and attached physician. There was much joy throughout the town when this greatly desirable object was attained. It was held to be the best possible measure for the young clergyman's welfare.

The new abode of the two friends was with a pious widow, of good social rank. The motherly care of the good widow assigned to Mr. Dimmesdale a front apartment, with a sunny exposure, and heavy window-curtains, to create a noontide shadow when desirable. On the other side of the house, old Roger Chillingworth arranged his study and laboratory. With such commodiousness of situation, these two learned persons sat themselves down, each in his own domain, yet familiarly passing from one apartment to the other, and bestowing a mutual and not incurious inspection into one another's business.

And the Reverend Arthur Dimmesdale's best discerning friends very reasonably imagined that the hand of Providence had done all this for the purpose of restoring the young minister to health. But another portion of the community had latterly begun to take its own view of the relation betwixt Mr. Dimmesdale and the mysterious old physician. Two or three individuals hinted that the man of skill, during his Indian captivity, had enlarged his medical attainments by joining in the incantations of the savage priests, who were universally acknowledged to be powerful enchanters, often performing seemingly miraculous cures by their skill in the black art. A large number affirmed that Roger Chillingworth's aspect had undergone a remarkable change while he had dwelt in town, and especially since his abode with Mr. Dimmesdale. At first, his expression had been calm, meditative, scholar-like. Now there was something ugly and evil in his face, which they had not previously noticed, and which grew still the more obvious to sight the oftener they looked upon him. According to the vulgar idea, the fire in his laboratory had been brought from the lower regions, and was fed with infernal fuel.

To sum up the matter, it grew to be a widely diffused opinion that the Rev. Arthur Dimmesdale was haunted either by Satan himself or Satan's emissary, in the guise of old Roger Chillingworth. The people looked, with an unshaken hope, to see the minister come forth out of the conflict transfigured with the glory which he would unquestionably win. Meanwhile, nevertheless, it was sad to think of the perchance mortal agony through which he must struggle towards his triumph.

Alas! To judge from the gloom and terror in the depth of the poor minister's eyes, the battle was a sore one, and the victory anything but secure.

CHAPTER 10: THE LEECH AND HIS PATIENT

Old Roger Chillingworth, throughout life, had been calm in temperament, a pure and upright man. He had begun an investigation with the severe and equal integrity of a judge instead of human passions, and wrongs inflicted on himself. But he now dug into the poor clergyman's heart, like a miner searching for gold. Sometimes a light glimmered out of the physician's eyes, burning blue and ominous. The soil where this dark miner was working had perchance shown indications that encouraged him.

"This man," said he, at one such moment, to himself, "pure as they deem him, all spiritual as he seems, hath inherited a strong animal nature from his father or his mother. Let us dig a little further in the direction of this vein!"

Then after long search into the minister's dim interior, and turning over many precious materials, in the shape of high aspirations for the welfare of his race, warm love of souls, pure sentiments, natural piety, strengthened by thought and study, and illuminated by revelation, all of which invaluable gold was perhaps no better than rubbish to the seeker, he would turn back, discouraged, and begin his quest towards another point. He groped along as stealthily, with as cautious a tread, and as wary an outlook, as a thief entering a chamber where a man lies only half asleep. In spite of his premeditated carefulness Mr. Dimmesdale would become vaguely aware that something inimical to his peace had thrust itself into relation with him.

Yet Mr. Dimmesdale would perhaps have seen this individual's character more perfectly, if a certain morbidness, to which sick hearts are liable, had not rendered him suspicious of all mankind. Trusting no man as his friend, he could not recognize his enemy when the latter actually appeared. He therefore still kept up a familiar intercourse with him.

One day, leaning his forehead on his hand, and his elbow on the sill of the open window, that looked towards the grave-yard, he talked with Roger Chillingworth, while the old man was examining a bundle of unsightly plants.

"Where," asked he, "my kind doctor, did you gather those herbs, with such a dark, flabby leaf?"

"Even in the graveyard here at hand," answered the physician, continuing his employment. "I found them growing on a grave. They grew out of his heart, and typify, it may be, some hideous secret that was buried with him, and which he had done better to confess during his lifetime."

"Perchance," said Mr. Dimmesdale, "he earnestly desired it, but could not."

"And wherefore?" rejoined the physician. "Wherefore not; since all the powers of nature call so earnestly for the confession of sin, that these black weeds have sprung up out of a buried heart, to make manifest, an outspoken crime?"

"That, good sir, is but a fantasy of yours," replied the minister. "There can be, if I forbode aright, no power, short of the Divine mercy, to disclose, whether by uttered words, or by type or emblem, the secrets that may be buried in the human heart. And, I conceive moreover, that the hearts holding such miserable secrets as you speak of, will yield them up, at that last day, not with reluctance, but with a joy unutterable."

"Then why not reveal it here?" asked Roger Chillingworth, glancing quietly aside at the minister. "Why should not the guilty ones sooner avail themselves of this unutterable solace?"

"They mostly do," said the clergyman, griping hard at his breast, as if afflicted with an importunate throb of pain. "Many, many a poor soul hath given its confidence to me, not only on the death-bed, but while strong in life, and fair in reputation."

"Yet some men bury their secrets thus," observed the calm physician.

"True; there are such men," answered Mr. Dimmesdale. "But not to suggest more obvious reasons, it may be that they are kept silent by the very constitution of their nature. Or, guilty as they may be, retaining, nevertheless, a zeal for God's glory and man's welfare, they shrink from displaying themselves black and filthy in the view of men; because, thenceforward, no good can be achieved by them. So, to their own unutterable torment, they go about among their fellow-creatures, looking pure as new-fallen snow, while their hearts are all speckled and spotted with iniquity of which they cannot rid themselves."

"These men deceive themselves," said Roger Chillingworth, with somewhat more emphasis than usual, and making a slight gesture with his forefinger. "They fear to take up the shame that rightfully belongs to them. But, if they seek to glorify God, let them not lift heavenward their unclean hands! Would thou have me to believe, O wise and pious friend, that a false show can be better, can be more for God's glory, or man' welfare, than God's own truth?"

They then heard the clear, wild laughter of a young child's voice, proceeding from the adjacent burial-ground. Looking instinctively from the open window, for it was summer-time, the minister beheld Hester Prynne and little Pearl passing along the footpath that traversed the enclosure. Pearl looked as beautiful as the day as she paused to gather the prickly burrs from a tall burdock which grew beside the tomb. Taking a handful of these, she arranged them along the lines of the scarlet letter that decorated the maternal bosom, to which the burrs, as their nature was, tenaciously adhered. Hester did not pluck them off.

Roger Chillingworth had by this time approached the window and smiled grimly down.

"There is no law, nor reverence for authority, no regard for human ordinances or opinions, right or wrong, mixed up with that child's composition," remarked he, as much to himself as to his companion. "I saw her, the other day, bespatter the Governor himself with water at the cattle-trough in Spring Lane. What, in heaven's name, is she? Is the imp altogether evil? Hath she any discoverable principle of being?"

"None, save the freedom of a broken law," answered Mr. Dimmesdale, in a quiet way, as if he had been discussing the point within himself, "Whether capable of good, I know not."

The child probably overheard their voices, for, looking up to the window with a bright, but naughty smile of mirth and intelligence, she threw one of the prickly burrs at the Rev. Mr. Dimmesdale. The sensitive clergyman shrank, with nervous dread, from the light missile. Detecting his emotion, Pearl clapped her little hands in the most extravagant ecstasy. Hester Prynne, likewise, had involuntarily looked up, and all these four persons, old and young, regarded one another in silence, till the child laughed aloud, and shouted—"Come away, mother! Come away, or yonder old black man will catch you! He hath got hold of the minister already. Come away, mother or he will catch you! But he cannot catch little Pearl!"

So she drew her mother away, skipping, dancing, and frisking fantastically among the hillocks of the dead people, like a creature that had nothing in common with a bygone and buried generation, nor owned herself akin to it.

"There goes a woman," resumed Roger Chillingworth, after a pause, "who, be her demerits what they may, hath none of that mystery of hidden sinfulness which you deem so grievous to be borne. Is Hester Prynne the less miserable, think you, for that scarlet letter on her breast?"

"I do verily believe it," answered the clergyman. "Nevertheless, I cannot answer for her. But still, methinks, it must needs be better for the sufferer to be free to show his pain, as this poor woman Hester is, than to cover it up in his heart."

"You would tell me, then, that I know all?" said Roger Chillingworth, deliberately, and fixing an eye, bright with intense and concentrated intelligence, on the minister's face. "Be it so! A bodily disease, which we look upon as whole and entire within itself, may, after all, be but a symptom of some ailment in the spiritual part."

"Then I need ask no further," said the clergyman, somewhat hastily rising from his chair. "You deal not, I take it, in medicine for the soul!"

"Thus, a sickness," continued Roger Chillingworth, going on, in an unaltered tone, without heeding the interruption, but standing up and confronting the emaciated and white-cheeked minister, with his low, dark, and misshapen figure," a sickness in your spirit hath immediately its appropriate manifestation in your bodily frame. How may this be unless you first lay open to him the wound or trouble in your soul?"

"No, not to thee! not to an earthly physician!" cried Mr. Dimmesdale, passionately, and turning his eyes, full and bright, and with a kind of fierceness, on old Roger Chillingworth. "Not to thee! But, if it be the soul's disease, then do I commit myself to the one Physician of the soul! He, if it stand with His good pleasure, can cure, or he can kill. Let Him do with me as, in His justice and wisdom, He shall see good. But who art thou, that meddlest in this matter? that dares thrust himself between the sufferer and his God?"

With a frantic gesture he rushed out of the room.

It proved not difficult to re-establish the intimacy of the two companions, on the same footing and in the same degree as heretofore. The young clergyman, after a few hours of privacy, was sensible that the disorder of his nerves had hurried him into an unseemly outbreak of temper. With these remorseful feelings, he lost no time in making the amplest apologies, and besought his friend still to continue the care.

It came to pass, not long after the scene above recorded, that the Reverend Mr. Dimmesdale, noon-day, and entirely unawares, fell into a deep, deep slumber, sitting in his chair and old Roger Chillingworth came into the room. The physician advanced directly in front of his patient, laid his hand upon his bosom, and thrust aside the vestment, that hitherto had always covered it even from the professional eye.

Then, indeed, Mr. Dimmesdale shuddered, and slightly stirred. After a brief pause, the physician turned away. But with what a wild look of wonder, joy, and horror! Had a man seen old Roger Chillingworth, at that moment of his ecstasy, he would have had no need to ask how

Satan comports himself when a precious human soul is lost to heaven, and won into his kingdom. But what distinguished the physician's ecstasy from Satan's was the trait of wonder in it!

CHAPTER 11: THE INTERIOR OF A HEART

After the incident last described, the intercourse between the clergyman and the physician was really of another character than it had previously been. The intellect of Roger Chillingworth had now a sufficiently plain path before it. There was a quiet depth of malice, hitherto latent, but active now, in this unfortunate old man, which led him to imagine a more intimate revenge than any mortal had ever wreaked upon an enemy.

Roger Chillingworth, however, was inclined to be hardly, if at all, less satisfied with the aspect of affairs. A revelation, he could almost say, had been granted to him. By its aid, in all the subsequent relations betwixt him and Mr. Dimmesdale, not merely the external presence, but the very inmost soul of the latter, seemed to be brought out before his eyes, so that he could see and comprehend its every movement. He became, thenceforth, not a spectator only, but a chief actor in the poor minister's interior world. He could play upon him as he chose.

All this was accomplished with a subtlety so perfect, that the minister, though he had constantly a dim perception of some evil influence watching over him, could never gain a knowledge of its actual nature. True, he looked doubtfully, fearfully, at the deformed figure of the old physician. It was impossible to assign a reason for such distrust and abhorrence, so Mr. Dimmesdale, conscious that the poison of one morbid spot was infecting his heart's entire substance, attributed all his presentiments to no other cause. He nevertheless, as a matter of principle, continued his habits of social familiarity with the old man, and thus gave him constant opportunities for perfecting the purpose to which the avenger had devoted himself.

While thus suffering under bodily disease, and gnawed and tortured by some black trouble of the soul, and given over to the machinations of his deadliest enemy, the Reverend Mr. Dimmesdale had achieved a brilliant popularity in his sacred office. He won it indeed, in great part, by his sorrows. His intellectual gifts, his moral perceptions, his power of experiencing and communicating emotion, were kept in a state of preternatural activity by the prick and anguish of his daily life. His fame, though still on its upward slope, already overshadowed the soberer reputations of his fellow-clergymen, eminent as several of them were.

They fancied him the mouth-piece of Heaven's messages of wisdom, and rebuke, and love. In their eyes, the very ground on which he trod was sanctified. The aged members of his flock, beholding Mr.

Dimmesdale's frame so feeble believed that he would go heavenward before them, and enjoined it upon their children that their old bones should be buried close to their young pastor's holy grave. And all this time, perchance, when poor Mr. Dimmesdale was thinking of his grave, he questioned with himself whether the grass would ever grow on it, because an accursed thing must there be buried!

It is inconceivable, the agony with which this public veneration tortured him. It was his genuine impulse to adore the truth. He longed to speak out from his own pulpit at the full height of his voice, and tell the people what he was. "I, whom you behold in these black garments of the priesthood, I, your pastor, whom you so reverence and trust, am utterly a pollution and a lie!"

More than once, Mr. Dimmesdale had gone into the pulpit, with a purpose never to come down its steps until he should have spoken words like the above. More than once he had actually spoken! But how? He had told his hearers that he was altogether vile, a viler companion of the vilest, the worst of sinners, an abomination, a thing of unimaginable iniquity, and that the only wonder was that they did not see his wretched body shriveled up before their eyes by the burning wrath of the Almighty! They heard it all, and did but reverence him the more. They little guessed what deadly purport lurked in those self-condemning words. "The godly youth!" said they among themselves. "The saint on earth! Alas! if he discern such sinfulness in his own white soul, what horrid spectacle would he behold in thine or mine!" The minister well knew the light in which his vague confession would be viewed. He had spoken the very truth, and transformed it into the veriest falsehood. And yet, by the constitution of his nature, he loved the truth, and loathed the lie, as few men ever did. Therefore, above all things else, he loathed his miserable self!

In Mr. Dimmesdale's secret closet, under lock and key, there was a bloody scourge. It was his custom, too, as it has been that of many other pious Puritans, to fast, not however, like them, in order to purify the body, and render it the fitter medium of celestial illumination, but rigorously, and until his knees trembled beneath him, as an act of penance. He kept vigils, likewise, night after night, sometimes in utter darkness. In these lengthened vigils visions seemed to flit before him. Now it was a herd of diabolic shapes, that grinned and mocked at the pale minister, and beckoned him away with them; now a group of shining angels, who flew upward heavily, as sorrow-laden, but grew more ethereal as they rose. And now, through the chamber which these spectral thoughts had made so ghastly, glided Hester Prynne leading along little Pearl, in her scarlet garb, and pointing her forefinger, first at the scarlet letter on her bosom, and then at the clergyman's own breast.

None of these visions ever quite deluded him. But, for all that, they were, in one sense, the truest and most substantial things which the poor minister now dealt with. To the untrue man, the whole universe is false and it shrinks to nothing within his grasp. And he himself in so far as he shows himself in a false light, becomes a shadow, or, indeed, ceases to exist. The only truth that continued to give Mr. Dimmesdale a real existence on this earth was the anguish in his inmost soul.

CHAPTER 12: THE MINISTER'S VIGIL

Mr. Dimmesdale reached the spot where, now so long since, Hester Prynne had lived through her first hours of public ignominy. The same platform or scaffold, black and weather-stained with the storm or sunshine of seven long years, and foot-worn, too, with the tread of many culprits who had since ascended it, remained standing beneath the balcony of the meeting-house. The minister went up the steps.

It was an obscure night in early May. No eye could see him. Why, then, had he come hither? He had been driven hither by the impulse of that Remorse which dogged him everywhere, and whose own sister and closely linked companion was that Cowardice which invariably drew him back. Poor, miserable man!

And thus, while standing on the scaffold, in this vain show of expiation, Mr. Dimmesdale was overcome with a great horror of mind, as if the universe were gazing at a scarlet token on his naked breast, right over his heart. Without any effort of his will, or power to restrain himself, he shrieked aloud: an outcry that went pealing through the night.

"It is done!" muttered the minister, covering his face with his hands. "The whole town will awake and hurry forth, and find me here!"

But it was not so. The town did not awake; or, if it did, the drowsy slumberers mistook the cry either for something frightful in a dream, or for the noise of witches. The clergyman, therefore, hearing no symptoms of disturbance, uncovered his eyes and looked about him. At one of the chamber-windows of Governor Bellingham's mansion, which stood at some distance, on the line of another street, he beheld the appearance of the old magistrate himself with a lamp in his hand a white night-cap on his head, and a long white gown enveloping his figure. The cry had evidently startled him. The magistrate, after a wary observation of the darkness, into which, nevertheless, he could see but little further than he might into a mill-stone, retired from the window.

The minister grew comparatively calm. His eyes, however, were soon greeted by a little glimmering light, which, at first a long way off was approaching up the street. As the light drew nearer, he beheld, within its illuminated circle, his brother clergyman, the Reverend Mr. Wilson, who, as Mr. Dimmesdale now conjectured, had been praying at the bedside of some dying man. And so he had. The good old minister came freshly from the death-chamber of Governor Winthrop, who had passed from earth to heaven within that very hour.

As the Reverend Mr. Wilson passed beside the scaffold the minister could hardly restrain himself from speaking. "A good evening to you, venerable Father Wilson. Come up hither, I pray you, and pass a pleasant hour with me!"

Good Heavens! Had Mr. Dimmesdale actually spoken? For one instant he believed that these words had passed his lips. But they were uttered only within his imagination. The venerable Father Wilson continued to step slowly onward and never once turning his head towards the guilty platform. When the light of the glimmering lantern had faded quite away, the minister discovered, by the faintness which came over him, that the last few moments had been a crisis of terrible anxiety, although his mind had made an involuntary effort to relieve itself by a kind of lurid playfulness.

Shortly afterwards he felt his limbs growing stiff with the unaccustomed chilliness of the night, and doubted whether he should be able to descend the steps of the scaffold. Morning would break and find him there. The neighborhood would begin to rouse itself. The earliest riser, coming forth in the dim twilight, would perceive a vaguely-defined figure aloft on the place of shame; and half-crazed betwixt alarm and curiosity, would go knocking from door to door, summoning all the people to behold the ghost. A dusky tumult would flap its wings from one house to another. Then old patriarchs would rise up in great haste, each in his flannel gown, and matronly dames, without pausing to put off their night-gear. All people, in a word, would come stumbling over their thresholds, and turning up their amazed and horror-stricken visages around the scaffold. Whom would they discern there, with the red eastern light upon his brow? Whom, but the Reverend Arthur Dimmesdale, half-frozen to death, overwhelmed with shame, and standing where Hester Prynne had stood!

Carried away by the grotesque horror of this picture, the minister, unawares, and to his own infinite alarm, burst into a great peal of laughter. It was immediately responded to by a light, airy, childish laugh, in which, with a thrill of the heart, but he knew not whether of exquisite pain, or pleasure as acute, he recognized the tones of little Pearl.

"Pearl! Little Pearl!" cried he, after a moment's pause; then, suppressing his voice, "Hester! Hester Prynne! Are you there?"

"Yes; it is Hester Prynne!" she replied, in a tone of surprise.

"Whence come you, Hester?" asked the minister. "What sent you hither?"

"I have been watching at a death-bed," answered Hester Prynne "at Governor Winthrop's death-bed, and have taken his measure for a robe, and am now going homeward to my dwelling."

"Come up hither, Hester, thou and little Pearl," said the Reverend Mr. Dimmesdale. "Come up hither once again, and we will stand all three together."

She silently ascended the steps, and stood on the platform, holding little Pearl by the hand. The minister felt for the child's other hand, and took it. The moment that he did so, there came what seemed a tumultuous rush of new life, other life than his own pouring like a torrent into his heart, and hurrying through all his veins, as if the mother and the child were communicating their vital warmth to his half-torpid system. The three formed an electric chain.

"Minister!" whispered little Pearl.

"What wouldst thou say, child?" asked Mr. Dimmesdale.

"Wilt thou stand here with mother and me, to-morrow noontide?" inquired Pearl.

"Nay; not so, my little Pearl," answered the minister; for, with the new energy of the moment, all the dread of public exposure, that had so long been the anguish of his life, had returned upon him; and he was already trembling at the conjunction in which, with a strange joy, nevertheless, he now found himself, "not so, my child. I shall, indeed, stand with thy mother and thee one other day, but not tomorrow."

"And what other time?" persisted the child.

"At the great judgment day," whispered the minister. Pearl laughed again.

But before Mr. Dimmesdale had done speaking, a light gleamed far and wide over all the muffled sky. It was doubtless caused by one of those meteors, which the night-watcher may so often observe burning out to waste, in the vacant regions of the atmosphere. So powerful was its radiance, that it thoroughly illuminated the dense medium of cloud betwixt the sky and earth. And there stood the minister, with his hand over his heart; and Hester Prynne, with the embroidered letter glimmering on her bosom; and little Pearl, herself a symbol, and the connecting link between those two. They stood in the noon of that strange and solemn splendor, as if it were the light that is to reveal all secrets, and the daybreak that shall unite all who belong to one another.

There was witchcraft in little Pearl's eyes; and her face, as she glanced upward at the minister, wore that naughty smile which made its expression frequently so elvish. She withdrew her hand from Mr.

Dimmesdale's, and pointed across the street. But he clasped both his hands over his breast, and cast his eyes towards the zenith.

Nothing was more common, in those days, than to interpret all meteoric appearances, and other natural phenomena that occurred with less regularity than the rise and set of sun and moon, as so many revelations from a supernatural source. But what shall we say, when an individual discovers a revelation addressed to himself alone, on the same vast sheet of record. In such a case, it could only be the symptom of a highly disordered mental state, when a man, rendered morbidly self-contemplative by long, intense, and secret pain, had extended his egotism over the whole expanse of nature.

To the disease in his own eye and heart, the minister, looking upward to the zenith, beheld there the appearance of an immense letter, the letter A, marked out in lines of dull red light. Not but the meteor may have shown itself at that point; burning duskily through a veil of cloud, but with no such shape as his guilty imagination gave it, or, at least, with so little definiteness, that another's guilt might have seen another symbol in it.

There was a singular circumstance that characterized Mr. Dimmesdale's psychological state at this moment. All the time that he gazed upward to the zenith, he was, nevertheless, perfectly aware that little Pearl was pointing her finger towards old Roger Chillingworth, who stood at no great distance from the scaffold. It might well be that the physician was not careful then, as at all other times, to hide the malevolence with which he looked upon his victim. Roger Chillingworth might have passed with them for the arch-fiend, standing there with a smile and scowl, to claim his own. So vivid was the expression, or so intense the minister's perception of it, that it seemed still to remain painted on the darkness after the meteor had vanished.

"Who is that man, Hester?" gasped Mr. Dimmesdale, overcome with terror. "I shiver at him! Dost thou know the man? I hate him, Hester!"

"Worthy sir," answered the physician, who had now advanced to the foot of the platform. "Pious Master Dimmesdale! can this be you? Well, well, indeed! We men of study, whose heads are in our books, have need to be straightly looked after! We dream in our waking moments, and walk in our sleep. Come, good sir, and my dear friend, I pray you let me lead you home!"

"How knewest thou that I was here?" asked the minister, fearfully.

"Verily, and in good faith," answered Roger Chillingworth, "I knew nothing of the matter. I had spent the better part of the night at the bedside of the worshipful Governor Winthrop, doing what my poor skill might to give him ease. Come with me, I beseech you, Reverend sir, else you will be poorly able to do Sabbath duty tomorrow."

"I will go home with you," said Mr. Dimmesdale.

With a chill despondency, like one awakening, all nerveless, from an ugly dream, he yielded himself to the physician, and was led away.

The next day, however, being the Sabbath, he preached a discourse which was held to be the richest and most powerful that had ever proceeded from his lips. But as he came down the pulpit steps, the grey-bearded sexton met him, holding up a black glove, which the minister recognized as his own.

"It was found," said the Sexton, "this morning on the scaffold where evil-doers are set up to public shame. Satan dropped it there!"

"Thank you, my good friend," said the minister, gravely, but startled at heart; for so confused was his remembrance, that he had almost brought himself to look at the events of the past night as visionary.

"Yes, it seems to be my glove, indeed!"

"And, since Satan saw fit to steal it, your reverence must needs handle him without gloves henceforward," remarked the old sexton, grimly smiling. "But did your reverence hear of the portent that was seen last night? a great red letter in the sky—the letter A, which we interpret to stand for Angel. For, as our good Governor Winthrop was made an angel this past night, it was doubtless held fit that there should be some notice thereof!"

"No," answered the minister. "I had not heard of it."

CHAPTER 13: ANOTHER VIEW OF HESTER

In her late singular interview with Mr. Dimmesdale, Hester Prynne was shocked at the condition to which she found the clergyman reduced. His nerve seemed absolutely destroyed. Knowing what this poor fallen man had once been, her whole soul was moved by the shuddering terror with which he had appealed to her, the outcast woman, for support against his instinctively discovered enemy. She decided, moreover, that he had a right to her utmost aid. Here was the iron link of mutual crime, which neither he nor she could break. Like all other ties, it brought along with it its obligations.

Hester Prynne did not now occupy precisely the same position in which we beheld her during the earlier periods of her ignominy. Years had come and gone. Pearl was now seven years old. Her mother, with the scarlet letter on her breast, glittering in its fantastic embroidery, had long been a familiar object to the townspeople. A species of general regard had ultimately grown up in reference to Hester Prynne. It is to the credit of human nature that, except where its selfishness is brought into play, it loves more readily than it hates. Hatred, by a gradual and quiet process, will even be transformed to love. She never battled with the public, but submitted uncomplainingly to its worst usage; she made no claim upon it in requital for what she suffered; she did not weigh upon its sympathies.

It was perceived, too, that while Hester never put forward even the humblest title to share in the world's privileges, further than to breathe the common air and earn daily bread for little Pearl and herself by the faithful labor of her hands, she was quick to acknowledge her sisterhood with the race of man whenever benefits were to be conferred. So ready was she to give of her little substance to every demand of poverty. None were so self-devoted as Hester when pestilence stalked through the town. In all seasons of calamity the outcast of society at once found her place. She came, not as a guest, but as a rightful inmate, into the household that was darkened by trouble. There glimmered the embroidered letter, with comfort in its unearthly ray. Elsewhere the token of sin, it was the taper of the sick chamber. Her breast, with its badge of shame, was but the softer pillow for the head that needed one. She was self-ordained a Sister of Mercy, or, we may rather say, the world's heavy hand had so ordained her, when neither the world nor she looked forward to this result. The letter was the symbol of her calling. Such helpfulness was found in her, so much power to do, and power to sympathize, that many people refused to interpret the scarlet A by its original signification. They said that it meant Abel, so strong was Hester Prynne, with a woman's strength.

The rulers, and the wise and learned men of the community, were longer in acknowledging the influence of Hester's good qualities than the people. The prejudices which they shared in common with the latter were fortified in themselves by an iron frame-work of reasoning, that made it a far tougher labor to expel them. Day by day, nevertheless, their sour and rigid wrinkles were relaxing into something which, in the due course of years, might grow to be an expression of almost benevolence. Individuals in private life, meanwhile, had quite forgiven Hester Prynne for her frailty; nay, more, they had begun to look upon the scarlet letter as the token, not of that one sin for which she had borne so long and dreary a penance, but of her many good deeds since.

The effect of the symbol, or rather, of the position in respect to society that was indicated by it, on the mind of Hester Prynne herself was powerful and peculiar. All the light and graceful foliage of her character had been withered up by this red-hot brand, and had long ago fallen away, leaving a bare and harsh outline, which might have been repulsive had she possessed friends or companions to be repelled by it. Even the attractiveness of her person had undergone a similar change. It was a sad transformation, too, that her rich and luxuriant hair had either been cut off, or was so completely hidden by a cap, that not a shining lock of it ever once gushed into the sunshine. It was due in part to all these causes, but still more to something else, that there seemed to be no longer anything in Hester's face for Love to dwell upon; nothing in Hester's bosom to make it ever again the pillow of Affection. Some attribute had departed from her, the permanence of which had been essential to keep her a woman.

Much of the marble coldness of Hester's impression was to be attributed to the circumstance that her life had turned, in a great measure, from passion and feeling to thought. Standing alone in the world she cast away the fragments of a broken chain. The world's law was no law for her mind. It was an age in which the human intellect, newly emancipated, had taken a more active and a wider range than for many centuries before. Hester Prynne imbibed this spirit. She assumed a freedom of speculation. In her lonesome cottage, by the seashore, thoughts visited her such as dared to enter no other dwelling in New England.

It is remarkable that persons who speculate the most boldly often conform with the most perfect quietude to the external regulations of society. The thought suffices them, without investing itself in the flesh and blood of action. So it seemed to be with Hester. Yet, had little Pearl never come to her from the spiritual world, it might have been far otherwise. Then she might have come down to us in history, hand in hand with Ann Hutchinson, as the foundress of a religious sect. But, in the education of her child, the mother's enthusiasm of thought had something to wreak itself upon.

Everything was against her. The world was hostile. The child's own nature had something wrong in it which continually betokened that she had been born amiss, the effluence of her mother's lawless passion, and often impelled Hester to ask, in bitterness of heart, whether it were for ill or good that the poor little creature had been born at all.

Indeed, the same dark question often rose into her mind with reference to the whole race of womanhood. Was existence worth accepting even to the happiest among them? She had long ago decided the whole system of society is to be torn down and built up anew. Then the very nature of the opposite sex, or its long hereditary habit, which has become like nature, is to be essentially modified before woman can be allowed to assume what seems a fair and suitable position. Finally, all other difficulties being obviated, woman cannot take advantage of these preliminary reforms until she herself shall have undergone a still mightier change, in which, perhaps, the ethereal essence, wherein she has her truest life, will be found to have evaporated. There was wild and ghastly scenery all around her, and a home and comfort nowhere. At times a fearful doubt strove to possess her soul, whether it were not better to send Pearl at once to Heaven, and go herself to such futurity as Eternal Justice should provide.

The scarlet letter had not done its office.

Now, however, her interview with the Reverend Mr. Dimmesdale, on the night of his vigil, had given her a new theme of reflection, and held up to her an object that appeared worthy of any exertion and sacrifice for its attainment. She had witnessed the intense misery beneath which the minister struggled. She saw that he stood on the verge of lunacy. A secret enemy had been continually by his side, under the semblance of a friend and helper. Hester could not but ask herself whether there had not originally been a defect of truth, courage, and loyalty on her own part, in allowing the minister to be thrown into a position where so much evil was to be foreboded when they had talked together in the prison-chamber.

Hester Prynne resolved to meet her former husband, and do what might be in her power for the rescue of the victim on whom he had so evidently set his gripe.

CHAPTER 14: HESTER AND THE PHYSICIAN

Hester bade little Pearl run down to the margin of the water and play with the shells and tangled sea-weed. Meanwhile her mother had accosted the physician. "I would speak a word with you," said she, "a word that concerns us much."

"Aha! and is it Mistress Hester that has a word for old Roger Chillingworth?" answered he, raising himself from his stooping posture. "With all my heart! Why, mistress, I hear good tidings of you on all hands! A magistrate, a wise and godly man, was discoursing of your affairs. It was debated whether or no, with safety to the commonweal, yonder scarlet letter might be taken off your bosom."

"It lies not in the pleasure of the magistrates to take off the badge," calmly replied Hester. "Were I worthy to be quit of it, it would fall away of its own nature, or be transformed into something that should speak a different purport."

"Nay, then, wear it, if it suit you better," rejoined he.

All this while Hester had been looking steadily at the old man and was shocked to discern what a change had been wrought upon him within the past seven years. It was not so much that he had grown older but the former aspect of an intellectual and studious man, calm and quiet, which was what she best remembered in him, had altogether vanished, and been succeeded by an eager, searching, almost fierce, yet carefully guarded look. It seemed to be his wish and purpose to mask this expression with a smile, but the latter played him false. The spectator could see his blackness. Ever and anon, too, there came a glare of red light out of his eyes, as if the old man's soul were on.

In a word, old Roger Chillingworth was a striking evidence of man's faculty of transforming himself into a devil. This unhappy person had effected such a transformation by devoting himself for seven years to the constant analysis of a heart full of torture, and deriving his enjoyment thence.

The scarlet letter burned on Hester Prynne's bosom. Here was another ruin, the responsibility of which came partly home to her.

"What see you in my face," asked the physician, "that you look at it so earnestly?"

"Something that would make me weep, if there were any tears bitter enough for it," answered she. "But let it pass! It is of yonder miserable man that I would speak."

"And what of him?" cried Roger Chillingworth, eagerly, as if he loved the topic, and were glad of an opportunity to discuss it with the only person of whom he could make a confidant.

"You tread behind his every footstep," said Hester, "You search his thoughts. You burrow and rankle in his heart! Your clutch is on his life, and you cause him to die daily a living death, and still he knows you not. In permitting this I have surely acted a false part by the only man to whom the power was left me to be true!"

"What choice had you?" asked Roger Chillingworth. "My finger, pointed at this man, would have hurled him from his pulpit into a dungeon, thence, peradventure, to the gallows!"

"It had been better so!" said Hester Prynne.

"What evil have I done the man?" asked Roger Chillingworth again. "But for my aid his life would have burned away in torments within the first two years after the perpetration of his crime and thine."

"Better he had died at once!" said Hester Prynne.

"Yea, woman, thou sayest truly!" cried old Roger Chillingworth, letting the lurid fire of his heart blaze out before her eyes. "Better had he died at once! Never did mortal suffer what this man has suffered. And all, all, in the sight of his worst enemy! He has been conscious of me. He has felt an influence dwelling always upon him like a curse. He knew, by some spiritual sense, for the Creator never made another being so sensitive as this, he knew that no friendly hand was pulling at his heartstrings, and that an eye was looking curiously into him, which sought only evil, and found it. But he knew not that the eye and hand were mine!"

The unfortunate physician, while uttering these words, lifted his hands with a look of horror, as if he had beheld some frightful shape, which he could not recognize, usurping the place of his own image in a glass.

"Hast thou not tortured him enough?" said Hester, noticing the old man's look. "Has he not paid thee all?"

"No, no! He has but increased the debt!" answered the physician, and as he proceeded, his manner lost its fiercer characteristics, and subsided into gloom. "Dost thou remember me, Hester, as I was nine years agone? All my life had been made up of earnest, studious, thoughtful, quiet years, bestowed faithfully for the increase of mine own knowledge, and faithfully, too, though this latter object was but casual to the other, faithfully for the advancement of human welfare."

"All this, and more," said Hester.

"And what am I now?" demanded he, looking into her face, and permitting the whole evil within him to be written on his features. "I have already told thee what I am. A fiend! Who made me so?"

"It was myself," cried Hester, shuddering. "It was I, not less than he. Why hast thou not avenged thyself on me?"

"I have left thee to the scarlet letter," replied Roger Chillingworth. "If that has not avenged me, I can do no more!"

He laid his finger on it with a smile.

"It has avenged thee!" answered Hester Prynne.

"I judged no less," said the physician. "And now what wouldst thou with me touching this man?"

"I must reveal the secret," answered Hester, firmly. "He must discern thee in thy true character. What may be the result I know not. There is no path to guide us out of this dismal maze."

"Woman, I could well-nigh pity thee," said Roger Chillingworth, unable to restrain a thrill of admiration too, for there was a quality almost majestic in the despair which she expressed. "I pity thee, for the good that has been wasted in thy nature."

"And I thee," answered Hester Prynne, "for the hatred that has transformed a wise and just man to a fiend!"

"Peace, Hester, peace!" replied the old man, with gloomy sternness. "By thy first step awry, thou didst plant the germ of evil; but since that moment it has all been a dark necessity. Let the black flower blossom as it may! Now, go thy ways, and deal as thou wilt with yonder man."

He waved his hand, and betook himself again to his employment of gathering herbs.

CHAPTER 15: HESTER AND PEARL

So Roger Chillingworth took leave of Hester Prynne, and went stooping away along the earth. Hester gazed after him a little while. She wondered what sort of herbs they were which the old man was so sedulous to gather. Did the sun, which shone so brightly everywhere else, really fall upon him? Or was there, as it rather seemed, a circle of ominous shadow moving along with his deformity whichever way he turned himself? And whither was he now going? Would he not suddenly sink into the earth, leaving a barren and blasted spot, where, in due course of time, would be seen deadly nightshade and whatever else of vegetable wickedness the climate could produce, all flourishing with hideous luxuriance? Or would he spread bat's wings and flee away, looking so much the uglier the higher he rose towards heaven?

"Be it sin or no," said Hester Prynne, bitterly, as still she gazed after him, "I hate the man!"

She marveled how she could ever have been wrought upon to marry him! She deemed it her crime most to be repented of, that she had ever endured and reciprocated the lukewarm grasp of his hand, and had suffered the smile of her lips and eyes to mingle and melt into his own. And it seemed a fouler offence committed by Roger Chillingworth than any which had since been done him, that, in the time when her heart knew no better, he had persuaded her to fancy herself happy by his side.

"Yes, I hate him!" repeated Hester more bitterly than before. "He betrayed me! He has done me worse wrong than I did him!"

Let men tremble to win the hand of woman, unless they win along with it the utmost passion of her heart! Else it may be their miserable fortune, as it was Roger Chillingworth's, when some mightier touch than their own may have awakened all her sensibilities. The emotion of that brief space, while she stood gazing after the crooked figure of old Roger Chillingworth, threw a dark light on Hester's state of mind, revealing much that she might not otherwise have acknowledged to herself.

He being gone, she summoned back her child. "Pearl! Little Pearl! Where are you?"

Pearl, whose activity of spirit never flagged, had been at no loss for amusement while her mother talked with the old gatherer of herbs. Perceiving a flock of beach-birds that fed and fluttered along the shore, the naughty child picked up her apron full of pebbles, and, creeping from rock to rock after these small sea-fowl, displayed remarkable dexterity in pelting them. One little gray bird, with a white breast, Pearl was almost sure had been hit by a pebble, and fluttered away with a broken wing. But then the elf-child sighed, and gave up her sport, because it grieved her to have done harm to a little being that was as wild as the sea-breeze, or as wild as Pearl herself.

Her final employment was to gather seaweed and thus assume the aspect of a little mermaid. As the last touch to her mermaid's garb, Pearl took some eel-grass and imitated, as best she could, on her own bosom the decoration with which she was so familiar on her mother's. A letter, the letter A, but freshly green instead of scarlet. The child bent her chin upon her breast, and contemplated this device with strange interest, even as if the one only thing for which she had been sent into the world was to make out its hidden import.

"I wonder if mother will ask me what it means?" thought Pearl. Just then she heard her mother's voice, and, flitting along as lightly as one of the little sea-birds, appeared before Hester Prynne dancing, laughing, and pointing her finger to the ornament upon her bosom.

"My little Pearl," said Hester, after a moment's silence, "the green letter, and on thy childish bosom, has no purport. But dost thou know, my child, what this letter means which thy mother is doomed to wear?"

"Yes, mother," said the child. "It is the great letter A."

"Dost thou know, child, wherefore thy mother wears this letter?"

"Truly do I!" answered Pearl, looking brightly into her mother's face. "It is for the same reason that the minister keeps his hand over his heart!"

"And what reason is that?" asked Hester, half smiling at the absurd incongruity of the child's observation; but on second thoughts turning pale. "What has the letter to do with any heart save mine?"

"Nay, mother, I have told all I know," said Pearl, more seriously than she was wont to speak. "Ask yonder old man whom thou hast been talking with, it may be he can tell. But in good earnest now, mother dear, what does this scarlet letter mean? And why dost thou wear it on thy bosom? And why does the minister keep his hand over his heart?"

She took her mother's hand in both her own, and gazed into her eyes with an earnestness that was seldom seen in her wild and capricious character. The thought occurred to Hester, that the child might really be seeking to approach her with childlike confidence, and doing what she could, and as intelligently as she knew how, to establish a meeting-point of sympathy. But now the idea came strongly into Hester's mind, that Pearl, with her remarkable precocity and acuteness, might already have approached the age when she could have been made a friend, and in trusted with as much of her mother's sorrows as could be imparted, without irreverence either to the parent or the child. In the little chaos of Pearl's character there might be seen emerging and could have been from the very first, the steadfast principles of an unflinching courage, an uncontrollable will, sturdy pride, which might be disciplined into self-respect, and a bitter scorn of many things which, when examined, might be found to have the taint of falsehood in them. With all these sterling attributes, thought Hester, the evil which she inherited from her mother must be great indeed, if a noble woman do not grow out of this elfish child.

If little Pearl were entertained with faith and trust, as a spirit messenger no less than an earthly child, might it not be her errand to soothe away the sorrow that lay cold in her mother's heart, and converted it into a tomb? And to help her to overcome the passion, once so wild, and even yet neither dead nor asleep, but only imprisoned within the same tomb-like heart?

Such were some of the thoughts that now stirred in Hester's mind, with as much vivacity of impression as if they had actually been whispered into her ear. And there was little Pearl, all this while, holding her mother's hand in both her own, and turning her face upward, while she put these searching questions, once and again, and still a third time.

"What does the letter mean, mother? and why dost thou wear it? and why does the minister keep his hand over his heart?"

"What shall I say?" thought Hester to herself. "No! if this be the price of the child's sympathy, I cannot pay it."

Then she spoke aloud. "Silly Pearl," said she, "what questions are these? There are many things in this world that a child must not ask about. What know I of the minister's heart? And as for the scarlet letter, I wear it for the sake of its gold thread."

"Mother," said she, "what does the scarlet letter mean?"

And the next morning, the first indication the child gave of being awake was by popping up her head from the pillow, and making that other enquiry, which she had so unaccountably connected with her investigations about the scarlet letter:

"Mother! Mother! Why does the minister keep his hand over his heart?"

"Hold thy tongue, naughty child!" answered her mother, with an asperity that she had never permitted to herself before. "Do not tease me; else I shall put thee into the dark closet!"

CHAPTER 16: A FOREST WALK

Hester Prynne remained constant in her resolve to make known to Mr. Dimmesdale, at whatever risk of present pain or ulterior consequences, the true character of the man who had crept into his intimacy. Hester never thought of meeting him in any narrower privacy than beneath the open sky.

At last, while attending a sick chamber, whither the Rev. Mr. Dimmesdale had been summoned to make a prayer, she learnt that he had gone, the day before, to visit the Apostle Eliot, among his Indian converts. Betimes, therefore, the next day, Hester took little Pearl, who was necessarily the companion of all her mother's expeditions, however inconvenient her presence, and set forth.

Overhead was a gray expanse of cloud, slightly stirred, however, by a breeze; so that a gleam of flickering sunshine might now and then be seen at its solitary play along the path. This flitting cheerfulness was always at the further extremity of some long vista through the forest. The sportive sunlight, feebly sportive, at best, in the predominant pensiveness of the day and scene, withdrew itself as they came nigh, and left the spots where it had danced the drearier, because they had hoped to find them bright.

"Mother," said little Pearl, "the sunshine does not love you. It runs away and hides itself, because it is afraid of something on your bosom." Pearl set forth at a great pace, and as Hester smiled to perceive, did actually catch the sunshine, and stood laughing in the midst of it.

"Come, my child!" said Hester, looking about her from the spot where Pearl had stood still in the sunshine. "We will sit down a little way within the wood, and rest ourselves."

"I am not weary, mother," replied the little girl. "But you may sit down, if you will tell me a story meanwhile."

"A story, child!" said Hester. "And about what?"

"Oh, a story about the Black Man," answered Pearl, taking hold of her mother's gown, and looking up, half earnestly, half mischievously, into her face. "How he haunts this forest, and carries a book with him a big. Didst thou ever meet the Black Man, mother?"

"And who told you this story, Pearl," asked her mother, recognizing a common superstition of the period.

"It was the old dame in the chimney corner, at the house where you watched last night," said the child. "And, mother, the old dame said that this scarlet letter was the Black Man's mark on thee. Is it true, mother?"

"Once in my life I met the Black Man!" said her mother. "This scarlet letter is his mark!"

Thus conversing, they entered sufficiently deep into the wood to secure themselves from the observation of any casual passenger along the forest track. Here they sat down on a luxuriant heap of moss near a brook flowing through the midst over a bed of fallen and drowned leaves. The brook kept up a babble, kind, quiet, soothing, but melancholy, like the voice of a young child that was spending its infancy without playfulness, and knew not how to be merry among sad acquaintance and events of somber hue.

Pearl resembled the brook, inasmuch as the current of her life gushed from a well-spring as mysterious, and had flowed through scenes shadowed as heavily with gloom. But, unlike the little stream, she danced and sparkled, and prattled airily along her course.

"What does this sad little brook say, mother?" inquired she.

"If thou hadst a sorrow of thine own, the brook might tell thee of it," answered her mother, "even as it is telling me of mine. But now, Pearl, I hear a footstep along the path, and the noise of one putting aside the branches. I would have thee betake thyself to play, and leave me to speak with him that comes yonder."

"Is it the Black Man?" asked Pearl.

"Go, silly child!" said her mother impatiently. "It is no Black Man! Thou canst see him now, through the trees. It is the minister!"

"And so it is!" said the child. "And, mother, he has his hand over his heart! Is it because, when the minister wrote his name in the book, the Black Man set his mark in that place? But why does he not wear it outside his bosom, as thou dost, mother?"

"Go now, child, and thou shalt tease me as thou wilt another time," cried Hester Prynne. "But do not stray far. Keep where thou canst hear the babble of the brook."

When her elf-child had departed, Hester Prynne made a step or two towards the track that led through the forest. She beheld the minister. He looked haggard and feeble. There was listlessness in his gait, as if he saw no reason for taking one step further, nor felt any desire to do so, but would have been glad, could he be glad of anything, to fling himself down at the root of the nearest tree, and lie there passive for evermore. To Hester's eye, the Reverend Mr. Dimmesdale exhibited no symptom of positive and vivacious suffering, except that, as little Pearl had remarked, he kept his hand over his heart.

CHAPTER 17: THE PASTOR AND HIS PARISHIONER

"Arthur Dimmesdale!" she said, faintly at first, then louder, but hoarsely, "Arthur Dimmesdale!"

"Who speaks?" answered the minister. He knew not whether it were a woman or a shadow. It may be that his pathway through life was haunted thus by a specter that had stolen out from among his thoughts. He made a step nearer, and discovered the scarlet letter.

"Hester! Hester Prynne!" said he, "is it thou? Art thou in life?"

"Even so." she answered. "In such life as has been mine these seven years past! And thou, Arthur Dimmesdale, dost thou yet live?"

It was no wonder that they thus questioned one another's actual and bodily existence, and even doubted of their own. So strangely did they meet in the dim wood that it was like the first encounter in the world beyond the grave of two spirits who had been intimately connected in their former life. Arthur Dimmesdale put forth his hand, chill as death, and touched the chill hand of Hester Prynne. They now felt themselves, at least, inhabitants of the same sphere.

Without a word more spoken they glided back into the shadow of the woods. When they found voice to speak, it was at first only to utter remarks and inquiries such as any two acquaintances might have made, about the gloomy sky, the threatening storm, and, next, the health of each. Thus they went onward, not boldly, but step by step, into the themes that were brooding deepest in their hearts. After awhile, the minister fixed his eyes on Hester Prynne's.

"Hester," said he, "hast thou found peace?"

She smiled drearily, looking down upon her bosom.

"Hast thou?" she asked.

"None. Nothing but despair!" he answered. "What else could I look for, being what I am, and leading such a life as mine? Were I an atheist I might have found peace long ere now. Hester, I am most miserable!"

"The people reverence thee," said Hester. "And surely thou workest good among them! Doth this bring thee no comfort?"

"More misery, Hester! Only the more misery!" answered the clergyman with a bitter smile. "As concerns the good which I may appear to do, I have no faith in it. What can a ruined soul like mine effect towards the redemption of other souls. I must stand up in my pulpit, and meet so many eyes turned upward to my face, as if the light of heaven were beaming from it! Must see my flock hungry for the truth and then look inward and discern the black reality of what they idolize? I have laughed, in bitterness and agony of heart, at the contrast between what I seem and what I am! And Satan laughs at it!"

"No, Hester, no!" replied the clergyman. "Happy are you, Hester, that wear the scarlet letter openly upon your bosom! Mine burns in secret! Thou little knowest what a relief it is, after the torment of a seven years' cheat, to look into an eye that recognizes me for what I am! Had I one friend, or were it my worst enemy, to whom, when sickened with the praises of all other men, I could daily betake myself, and be known as the vilest of all sinners, methinks my soul might keep itself alive thereby. Even thus much of truth would save me!"

Hester Prynne looked into his face, but hesitated to speak. His words here offered her the very point of circumstances in which to interpose what she came to say. She conquered her fears, and spoke: "Thou hast long had such an enemy, and dwellest with him, under the same roof!"

The minister started to his feet, gasping for breath, and clutching at his heart, as if he would have torn it out of his bosom.

She now read his heart more accurately. She doubted not that the continual presence of Roger Chillingworth, the secret poison of his malignity, infecting all the air about him, and his authorized interference, as a physician, with the minister's physical and spiritual infirmities, that these bad opportunities had been turned to a cruel purpose. By means of them, the sufferer's conscience had been kept in an irritated state, the tendency of which was, not to cure by wholesome pain, but to disorganize and corrupt his spiritual being. Its result, on earth, could hardly fail to be insanity, and hereafter, that eternal alienation from the Good and True, of which madness is perhaps the earthly type.

Such was the ruin to which she had brought the man that she still so passionately loved! And now, rather than have had this grievous wrong to confess, she would gladly have laid down on the forest leaves, and died there, at Arthur Dimmesdale's feet.

"Oh, Arthur!" cried she, "forgive me! That old man! The physician! He whom they call Roger Chillingworth! He was my husband!"

The minister looked at her for an instant, with all that violence of passion. Never was there a blacker or a fiercer frown than Hester now encountered. For the brief space that it lasted, it was a dark transfiguration. He sank down on the ground, and buried his face in his hands.

"I might have known it," murmured he. "Oh, Hester Prynne, thou little, little knowest all the horror of this thing! The horrible ugliness of this exposure of a sick and guilty heart to the very eye that would gloat over it! Woman, woman, thou art accountable for this! I cannot forgive thee!"

"Thou shalt forgive me!" cried Hester, flinging herself on the fallen leaves beside him. "Let God punish! Thou shalt forgive!"

With sudden and desperate tenderness she threw her arms around him, and pressed his head against her bosom. Hester would not set him free, lest he should look her sternly in the face. All the world had frowned on her and still she bore it all. Heaven, likewise, had frowned upon her, and she had not died. But the frown of this pale, weak, sinful, and sorrow-stricken man was what Hester could not bear, and live!

"Wilt thou yet forgive me?" she repeated, over and over again. "Wilt thou not frown? Wilt thou forgive?"

"I do forgive you, Hester," replied the minister at length, with a deep utterance, out of an abyss of sadness, but no anger. "We are not, Hester, the worst sinners in the world. There is one worse than even the polluted priest! That old man's revenge has been blacker than my sin. He has violated, in cold blood, the sanctity of a human heart. Thou and I, Hester, never did so!"

"Never, never!" whispered she. "What we did had a consecration of its own. We felt it so! Hast thou forgotten it?"

"Hush, Hester!" said Arthur Dimmesdale, rising from the ground. "No; I have not forgotten!"

How dreary looked the forest-track that led backward to the settlement, where Hester Prynne must take up again the burden of her ignominy and the minister the hollow mockery of his good name! Here seen only by his eyes, the scarlet letter need not burn into the bosom of the fallen woman! Here seen only by her eyes, Arthur Dimmesdale, false to God and man, might be, for one moment true! He started at a thought that suddenly occurred to him.

"Hester!" cried he, "here is a new horror! Roger Chillingworth knows your purpose to reveal his true character. Will he continue, then, to keep our secret? What will now be the course of his revenge?"

"There is a strange secrecy in his nature," replied Hester, thoughtfully; "I deem it not likely that he will betray the secret."

"And I! How am I to live longer, breathing the same air with this deadly enemy?" exclaimed Arthur Dimmesdale, shrinking within himself, and pressing his hand nervously against his heart, a gesture that had grown involuntary with him. "Think for me, Hester! Thou art strong. Resolve for me!"

"Thou must dwell no longer with this man," said Hester, slowly and firmly.

"The judgment of God is on me," answered the conscience-stricken priest. "It is too mighty for me to struggle with!"

"Heaven would show mercy," rejoined Hester, "hadst thou but the strength to take advantage of it."

"Be thou strong for me!" answered he. "Advise me what to do."

"Is the world, then, so narrow?" exclaimed Hester Prynne, fixing her deep eyes on the minister's, and instinctively exercising a magnetic power over a spirit so shattered and subdued that it could hardly hold itself erect. "Doth the universe lie within the compass of yonder town, which only a little time ago was but a leaf-strewn desert, as lonely as this around us? Backward to the settlement, thou sayest! Yes; but, onward, too! So brief a journey would bring thee from a world where thou hast been most wretched, to one where thou mayest still be happy! Is there not shade enough in all this boundless forest to hide thy heart from the gaze of Roger Chillingworth?"

"It cannot be!" answered the minister. "I am powerless to go. I dare not quit my post, though an unfaithful sentinel, whose sure reward is death and dishonor, when his dreary watch shall come to an end!"

"Thou art crushed under this seven years' weight of misery," replied Hester, fervently resolved to buoy him up with her own energy. "But thou shalt leave it all behind thee! Leave this wreck and ruin here where it hath happened! Begin all anew! The future is yet full of trial and success. There is happiness to be enjoyed! There is good to be done! Preach! Write! Act! Do anything, save to lie down and die!"

"Oh, Hester!" cried Arthur Dimmesdale, in whose eyes a fitful light, kindled by her enthusiasm, flashed up and died away, "thou tellest of running a race to a man whose knees are tottering beneath him! I must die here! There is not the strength or courage left me to venture into the wide, strange, difficult world alone!"

It was the last expression of the despondency of a broken spirit. He lacked energy to grasp the better fortune that seemed within his reach.

He repeated the word. "Alone, Hester!"

"Thou shall not go alone!" answered she, in a deep whisper. Then, all was spoken!

CHAPTER 18: A FLOOD OF SUNSHINE

Arthur Dimmesdale gazed into Hester's face with a look in which hope and joy shone out, indeed, but with fear betwixt them, and a kind of horror at her boldness, who had spoken what he vaguely hinted at, but dared not speak.

But Hester Prynne, with a mind of native courage and activity, and outlawed from society, had habituated herself to such latitude of speculation as was altogether foreign to the clergyman. She had wandered, without rule or guidance, in a moral wilderness. For years past she had looked from this estranged point of view at human institutions, criticizing all. The scarlet letter was her passport into regions where other women dared not tread. Shame, Despair, Solitude! These had been her teachers, stern and wild ones, and they had made her strong, but taught her much amiss.

The minister, on the other hand, had never gone through an experience calculated to lead him beyond the scope of generally received laws; although, in a single instance, he had so fearfully transgressed one of the most sacred of them. But this had been a sin of passion. As a priest, the framework of his order inevitably hemmed him in.

Thus we seem to see that, as regarded Hester Prynne, the whole seven years of outlaw and ignominy had been little other than a preparation for this very hour. But Arthur Dimmesdale! He was broken down by long and exquisite suffering; that his mind was darkened and confused by the very remorse which harrowed it; that, between fleeing as an avowed criminal, and remaining as a hypocrite, conscience might find it hard to strike the balance; that, finally, to this poor pilgrim, on his dreary and desert path, faint, sick, miserable, there appeared a glimpse of human affection and sympathy, a new life, and a true one, in exchange for the heavy doom which he was now expiating.

The struggle, if there were one, need not be described. Let it suffice that the clergyman resolved to flee, and not alone.

Thought he, "If if this be the path to a better life, as Hester would persuade me, I surely give up no fairer prospect by pursuing it! Neither can I any longer live without her companionship; so powerful is she to sustain, so tender to soothe! O Thou to whom I dare not lift mine eyes, wilt Thou yet pardon me?"

"Thou wilt go", said Hester calmly, as he met her glance.

The decision once made, a glow of strange enjoyment threw its flickering brightness over the trouble of his breast. His spirit rose, as it were, with a bound, and attained a nearer prospect of the sky, than throughout all the misery which had kept him groveling on the earth.

"Do I feel joy again?" cried he, wondering at himself. "Oh, Hester, thou art my better angel! This is already the better life! Why did we not find it sooner?"

"Let us not look back," answered Hester Prynne. "The past is gone! See! With this symbol I undo it all, and make it as if it had never been!"

So speaking, she undid the clasp that fastened the scarlet letter, and, taking it from her bosom, threw it to a distance among the withered leaves. There lay the embroidered letter, glittering like a lost jewel, which some ill-fated wanderer might pick up, and thenceforth be haunted by strange phantoms of guilt, sinkings of the heart, and unaccountable misfortune.

The stigma gone, Hester heaved a long, deep sigh, in which the burden of shame and anguish departed from her spirit. By another impulse, she took off the formal cap that confined her hair, and down it fell upon her shoulders, dark and rich, with at once a shadow and a light in its abundance, and imparting the charm of softness to her features. There played around her mouth, and beamed out of her eyes, a radiant and tender smile, that seemed gushing from the very heart of womanhood. A crimson flush was glowing on her cheek, that had been long so pale. All at once, as with a sudden smile of heaven, forth burst the sunshine, pouring a very flood into the obscure forest, gladdening each green leaf, transmuting the yellow fallen ones to gold, and gleaming adown the gray trunks of the solemn trees. The objects that had made a shadow hitherto, embodied the brightness now. The course of the little brook might be traced by its merry gleam afar into the wood's heart of mystery, which had become a mystery of joy.

Love, whether newly-born, or aroused from a death-like slumber, must always create a sunshine, filling the heart so full of radiance, that it overflows upon the outward world.

Hester looked at him with a thrill of another joy. "Thou must know Pearl!" said she. "Thou wilt see her now with other eyes. Thou wilt love her dearly, as I do, and wilt advise me how to deal with her!"

"Dost thou think the child will be glad to know me?" asked the minister, somewhat uneasily.

"Ah, that was sad!" answered the mother. "But she will love thee dearly, and thou her. She is not far off. I will call her. Pearl! Pearl!"

Hester smiled, and again called to Pearl, who was visible at some distance. She heard her mother's voice, and approached slowly through the forest.

Pearl had not found the hour pass wearisomely while her mother sat talking with the clergyman. The great black forest became the playmate of the lonely infant, as well as it knew how. Somber as it was, it put on the kindest of its moods to welcome her. The mother-forest, and these wild things which it nourished, all recognized a kindred wilderness in the human child. And she was gentler here than in the grassy-margined streets of the settlement, or in her mother's cottage. The flowers appeared to know it. Pearl gathered the violets. With these she decorated her hair and her young waist, and became a nymph child. In such guise had Pearl adorned herself, when she heard her mother's voice, and came slowly back.

Slowly; for she saw the clergyman!

CHAPTER 19: THE CHILD AT THE BROOKSIDE

"Thou wilt love her dearly," repeated Hester Prynne, as she and the minister sat watching little Pearl. "Dost thou not think her beautiful? But I know whose brow she has!"

"Dost thou know, Hester," said Arthur Dimmesdale, with an unquiet smile, "that this dear child, tripping about always at thy side, hath caused me many an alarm? Methought that my own features were partly repeated in her face, and so strikingly that the world might see them!"

It was with a feeling which neither of them had ever before experienced, that they sat and watched Pearl's slow advance. In her was visible the tie that united them. And Pearl was the oneness of their being. Be the foregone evil what it might, how could they doubt that their earthly lives and future destinies were conjoined. Thoughts like these, and perhaps other thoughts, which they did not acknowledge or define, threw an awe about the child as she came onward.

"Let her see nothing strange," whispered Hester. "she is seldom tolerant of emotion when she does not fully comprehend the why and wherefore. She loves me, and will love thee!"

"Thou canst not think," said the minister, glancing aside at Hester Prynne, "how my heart dreads this interview, and yearns for it! But, in truth children are not readily won to be familiar with me."

By this time Pearl had reached the margin of the brook, and stood on the further side, gazing silently at Hester and the clergyman. Hester felt herself, in some indistinct and tantalizing manner, estranged from Pearl, as if the child, in her lonely ramble through the forest, had strayed out of the sphere in which she and her mother dwelt together, and was now vainly seeking to return to it.

There were both truth and error in the impression; the child and mother were estranged, but through Hester's fault, not Pearl's. Since the latter rambled from her side, another inmate had been admitted within the circle of the mother's feelings, and so modified the aspect of them all, that Pearl, the returning wanderer, could not find her wonted place, and hardly knew where she was.

"I have a strange fancy," observed the sensitive minister, "that this brook is the boundary between two worlds, and that thou canst never meet thy Pearl again. Pray hasten her, for this delay has already imparted a tremor to my nerves."

"Come, dearest child!" said Hester encouragingly, and stretching out both her arms. "How slow thou art! Leap across the brook and come to us. Thou canst leap like a young deer!"

Pearl, without responding in any manner to these honey-sweet expressions, remained on the other side of the brook. Now she fixed her bright wild eyes on her mother, now on the minister, and now included them both in the same glance, as if to detect and explain to herself the relation which they bore to one another. For some unaccountable reason, as Arthur Dimmesdale felt the child's eyes upon himself, his hand stole over his heart. Pearl stretched out her hand, with the small forefinger extended, and pointing evidently towards her mother's breast.

"Thou strange child! why dost thou not come to me?" exclaimed Hester. "Leap across the brook, naughty child, and run hither! Else I must come to thee!"

But Pearl, not a whit startled at her mother's threats any more than mollified by her entreaties, now suddenly burst into a fit of passion, gesticulating violently, and throwing her small figure into the most extravagant contortions. She accompanied this wild outbreak with piercing shrieks.

"I see what ails the child," whispered Hester to the clergyman, and turning pale in spite of a strong effort to conceal her trouble and annoyance.

"I pray you," answered the minister, "if thou hast any means of pacifying the child, do it forthwith!"

"Pearl," said she sadly, "look down at thy feet! There! Before thee! On the hither side of the brook!" The child turned her eyes to the point indicated; and there lay the scarlet letter.

"Bring it hither!" said Hester.

"Come thou and take it up!" answered Pearl.

"Was ever such a child!" observed Hester aside to the minister. "But, in very truth, she is right as regards this hateful token. I must bear its torture yet a little longer until we shall have left this region, and look back hither as to a land which we have dreamed of."

With these words she advanced to the margin of the brook, took up the scarlet letter, and fastened it again into her bosom. There was a sense of inevitable doom upon her as she thus received back this deadly symbol from the hand of fate. As if there were a withering spell in the sad letter, her beauty, the warmth and richness of her womanhood, departed like fading sunshine, and a gray shadow seemed to fall across her. When the dreary change was wrought, she extended her hand to Pearl.

"Dost thou know thy mother now, child?", asked she, reproachfully, but with a subdued tone.

"Yes;" answered the child, bounding across the brook, and clasping Hester in her arms "Now thou art my mother indeed! and I am thy little Pearl!"

She drew down her mother's head, and kissed her brow and both her cheeks. But then Pearl put up her mouth and kissed the scarlet letter, too.

"That was not kind!" said Hester. "When thou hast shown me a little love, thou mockest me!"

"Why doth the minister sit yonder?" asked Pearl.

"He waits to welcome thee," replied her mother. "He loves thee, my little Pearl, and loves thy mother, too. Wilt thou not love him?"

"Doth he love us?" said Pearl, looking up with acute intelligence into her mother's face. "Will he go back with us, hand in hand, we three together, into the town?"

"Not now, my child," answered Hester. "But in days to come he will walk hand in hand with us."

"And will he always keep his hand over his heart?" inquired Pearl.

"Foolish child, what a question is that!" exclaimed her mother. "Come, and ask his blessing!"

But, whether influenced by the jealousy that seems instinctive with every petted child towards a dangerous rival, or from whatever caprice of her freakish nature, Pearl would show no favor to the clergyman. The minister, painfully embarrassed, but hoping that a kiss might prove a talisman to admit him into the child's kindlier regards, bent forward, and impressed one on her brow. Hereupon, Pearl broke away from her mother, and, running to the brook, stooped over it, and bathed her forehead, until the unwelcome kiss was quite washed off. She then remained apart, silently watching Hester and the clergyman; while they talked together and made such arrangements as were suggested by their new position and the purposes soon to be fulfilled.

And now this fateful interview had come to a close. And the melancholy brook would add this other tale to the mystery with which its little heart was already overburdened, and whereof it still kept up a murmuring babble, with not a whit more cheerfulness of tone than for ages heretofore.

CHAPTER 20: THE MINISTER IN A MAZE

As the minister departed, in advance of Hester Prynne and little Pearl, he threw a backward glance, half expecting that he should discover only some faintly traced features or outline of the mother and the child. So great a vicissitude in his life could not at once be received as real. But there was Hester. And there was Pearl, too, lightly dancing from the margin of the brook. So the minister had not fallen asleep and dreamed!

He recalled and more thoroughly defined the plans which Hester and himself had sketched for their departure. It had been determined between them that the Old World offered them a more eligible shelter and concealment than the wilds of New England or all America. Not to speak of the clergyman's health, so inadequate to sustain the hardships of a forest life, his native gifts, his culture, and his entire development would secure him a home only in the midst of civilization and refinement. It so happened that a ship lay in the harbor. This vessel had recently arrived from the Spanish Main, and within three days' time would sail for Bristol. Hester Prynne, whose vocation, as a self-enlisted Sister of Charity, had brought her acquainted with the captain and crew, could take upon herself to secure the passage of two individuals and a child with all the secrecy which circumstances rendered more than desirable.

The minister had inquired of Hester, with no little interest, the precise time at which the vessel might be expected to depart. It would probably be on the fourth day from the present. On the third day from the present he was to preach the Election Sermon; and he could not have chanced upon a more suitable mode and time of terminating his professional career. "At least, they shall say of me," thought this exemplary man, "that I leave no public duty unperformed or ill-performed!" No man, for any considerable period, can wear one face to himself and another to the multitude, without finally getting bewildered as to which may be the true.

The excitement of Mr. Dimmesdale's feelings as he returned from his interview with Hester, lent him unaccustomed physical energy, and hurried him townward at a rapid pace. The pathway among the woods seemed wilder than he remembered it on his outward journey. But he overcame all the difficulties of the track. He could not but recall how feebly, and with what frequent pauses for breath he had toiled over the same ground, only two days before. As he drew near the town, he took an impression of change from the series of familiar objects that presented themselves. There, indeed, was each former trace of the street, as he remembered it. Not the less, however, came this importunately obtrusive sense of change. The same was true as regarded the acquaintances whom he met. They looked neither older nor younger; it was impossible to describe in what respect they differed from the individuals on whom he had so recently bestowed a parting glance; and yet the minister's deepest sense seemed to inform him of their mutability. A similar impression struck him most remarkably as he passed under the walls of his own church. The edifice had so very strange, and yet so familiar an aspect, that Mr. Dimmesdale's mind vibrated between two ideas; either that he had seen it only in a dream hitherto, or that he was merely dreaming about it now.

The minister's own will, and Hester's will, and the fate that grew between them, had wrought this transformation. It was the same town as heretofore, but the same minister returned not from the forest. He might have said to the friends who greeted him, "I am not the man for whom you take me! I left him yonder in the forest!"

Before Mr. Dimmesdale reached home, his inner man gave him other evidences of a revolution in the sphere of thought and feeling. At every step he was incited to do some strange, wild, wicked thing or other, with a sense that it would be at once involuntary and intentional, in spite of himself, yet growing out of a profounder self than that which opposed the impulse. For instance, he met one of his own deacons. Now, during a conversation of some two or three moments between the Reverend Mr. Dimmesdale and this excellent and hoary-bearded deacon, it was only by the most careful self-control that the former could refrain from uttering certain blasphemous suggestions that rose into his mind, respecting the communion-supper. He absolutely trembled and turned pale as ashes. And, even with this terror in his heart, he could hardly avoid laughing, to imagine how the sanctified old patriarchal deacon would have been petrified by his minister's impiety.

Again, another incident of the same nature. Hurrying along the street, the Reverend Mr. Dimmesdale encountered the eldest female member of his church. The good grandam's chief earthly comfort was to meet her pastor, whether casually, or of set purpose, and be refreshed with a word of warm, fragrant, heaven-breathing Gospel truth, from his beloved lips, into her dulled, but rapturously attentive ear. But, on this occasion, up to the moment of putting his lips to the old woman's ear, Mr. Dimmesdale could recall no text of Scripture. What he really did whisper, the minister could never afterwards recollect.

Again, a third instance. After parting from the old church member, he met the youngest sister of them all. She was fair and pure as a lily that had bloomed in Paradise. Satan, that afternoon, had surely led the poor young girl away from her mother's side, and thrown her into the pathway of this sorely tempted, lost and desperate man. Such was his sense of power over this virgin soul, trusting him as she did, that the minister felt potent to blight all the field of innocence with but one wicked look, and develop all its opposite with but a word. So, with a mightier struggle than he had yet sustained, he held his Geneva cloak before his face, and hurried onward, making no sign of recognition, and leaving the young sister to digest his rudeness as she might. She ransacked her conscience and took herself to task, poor thing, for a thousand imaginary faults, and went about her household duties with swollen eyelids the next morning.

Before the minister had time to celebrate his victory over this last temptation, he was conscious of another impulse, more ludicrous, and almost as horrible. It was to stop short in the road, and teach some very wicked words to a knot of little Puritan children who were playing there, and had but just begun to talk. Denying himself this freak he met a drunken seaman, one of the ship's crew from the Spanish Main. And here, since he had so valiantly forborne all other wickedness, poor Mr. Dimmesdale longed at least to shake hands with the tarry black-guard, and recreate himself with a few improper jests, such as dissolute sailors so abound with, and a volley of good, round, solid, satisfactory, and heaven-defying oaths!

"What is it that haunts and tempts me thus?" cried the minister to himself, at length, pausing in the street, and striking his hand against his forehead. "Am I mad?"

At the moment when the Reverend Mr. Dimmesdale thus communed with himself, and struck his forehead with his hand, old Mistress Hibbins, the reputed witch-lady, is said to have been passing by. She came to a full stop, looked shrewdly into his face, smiled craftily, and, though little given to converse with clergymen, began a conversation.

"So, reverend sir, you have made a visit into the forest," observed the witch-lady, nodding her high head-dress at him. "The next time I pray you to allow me only a fair warning. My good word will go far towards gaining any strange gentleman a fair reception from yonder potentate you wot of!"

"I profess, madam," answered the clergyman, with a grave obeisance, such as the lady's rank demanded, and his own good breeding made imperative, "I went not into the forest to seek a potentate. My one sufficient object was to greet that pious friend of mine, the Apostle

Eliot, and rejoice with him over the many precious souls he hath won from heathendom!"

"Ha, ha, ha!" cackled the old witch-lady, still nodding her high head-dress at the minister. "Well, well! We must needs talk thus in the daytime! But at midnight, and in the forest, we shall have other talk together!" She passed on with her aged stateliness, but often turning back her head and smiling at him, like one willing to recognize a secret intimacy of connection.

"Have I then sold myself," thought the minister, "to the fiend?"

The wretched minister! He had made a bargain very like it! Tempted by a dream of happiness, he had yielded himself with deliberate choice, as he had never done before, to what he knew was deadly sin. And the infectious poison of that sin had been thus rapidly diffused throughout his moral system.

He had by this time reached his dwelling on the edge of the burial ground, and, hastening up the stairs, took refuge in his study. He entered the accustomed room, and looked around him on its books, its windows, its fireplace, and the tapestried comfort of the walls, with the same perception of strangeness that had haunted him throughout his walk from the forest dell into the town and thitherward. He seemed to stand apart, and eye this former self with scornful pitying, but half envious curiosity. That self was gone. Another man had returned out of the forest, a wiser one, with a knowledge of hidden mysteries which the simplicity of the former never could have reached. A bitter kind of knowledge that!

While occupied with these reflections, a knock came at the door of the study, and the minister said, "Come in!", not wholly devoid of an idea that he might behold an evil spirit. And so he did! It was old Roger Chillingworth that entered. The minister stood white and speechless, with one hand on the Hebrew Scriptures, and the other spread upon his breast.

"Welcome home, reverend sir," said the physician "Dear sir, you look pale. Will not my aid be requisite to put you in heart and strength to preach your Election Sermon?"

"Nay, I think not so," rejoined the Reverend Mr. Dimmesdale. "I think to need no more of your drugs, my kind physician, good though they be, and administered by a friendly hand."

All this time Roger Chillingworth was looking at the minister with the grave and intent regard of a physician towards his patient. But, in spite of this outward show, the latter was almost convinced of the old man's knowledge, or, at least, his confident suspicion, with respect to his own interview with Hester Prynne. The physician knew then that in the minister's regard he was no longer a trusted friend, but his bitterest enemy. So much being known, it would appear natural that a part of it should be expressed. It is singular, however, how long a time often passes before words embody things; and with what security two persons, who choose to avoid a certain subject, may approach its very verge, and retire without disturbing it. Thus the minister felt no apprehension that Roger Chillingworth would touch, in express words, upon the real position which they sustained towards one another. Yet did the physician, in his dark way, creep frightfully near the secret.

"Were it not better," said he, "that you use my poor skill tonight? The people look for great things from you, apprehending that another year may come about and find their pastor gone."

"Yes, to another world," replied the minister with pious resignation. "But touching your medicine, kind sir, in my present frame of body I need it not."

"I joy to hear it," answered the physician. And he took his leave.

Left alone, the minister summoned a servant of the house, and requested food. Then flinging the already written pages of the Election Sermon into the fire, he forthwith began another, which he wrote with such an impulsive flow of thought and emotion, that he fancied himself inspired. The night fled away. Morning came and at last sunrise threw a golden beam into the study, and laid it right across the minister's bedazzled eyes. There he was, with the pen still between his fingers, and a vast, immeasurable tract of written space behind him!

CHAPTER 21: THE NEW ENGLAND HOLIDAY

On this public holiday, the morning of the day on which the new Governor was to receive his office, Hester was clad in a garment of coarse gray cloth. It had the effect of making her fade personally out of sight and outline; while again the scarlet letter brought her back from this twilight indistinctness. Her face, so long familiar to the townspeople, showed the marble quietude which they were accustomed to behold there. It was like the frozen calmness of a dead woman's features; owing this dreary resemblance to the fact that Hester was actually dead, in respect to any claim of sympathy.

It might be, on this one day, that there was an expression unseen before, nor, indeed, vivid enough to be detected now. "Look your last on the scarlet letter and its wearer!", the people's victim and lifelong bond-slave, as they fancied her, might say to them. "Yet a little while, and she will be beyond your reach! A few hours longer and the deep, mysterious ocean will quench and hide forever the symbol which ye have caused to burn on her bosom!"

Pearl was decked out with airy gaiety. Her garb was all of one idea with her nature. On this eventful day, moreover, there was a certain singular inquietude and excitement in her mood, resembling nothing so much as the shimmer of a diamond, that sparkles and flashes with the varied throbbings of the breast on which it is displayed. Children have always a sympathy in the agitations of those connected with them: always, especially, a sense of any trouble or impending revolution, of whatever kind, in domestic circumstances; and therefore Pearl, who was the gem on her mother's unquiet bosom, betrayed, by the very dance of her spirits, the emotions which none could detect in the marble passiveness of Hester's brow.

"Why, what is this, mother?" cried she. "Wherefore have all the people left their work to-day? Is it a play-day for the whole world?"

"They wait to see the procession pass," said Hester. "For the Governor and the magistrates are to go by, and the ministers, and all the great people and good people, with the music and the soldiers marching before them."

"And will the minister be there?" asked Pearl. "And will he hold out both his hands to me, as when thou ledst me to him from the brook-side?"

"He will be there, child," answered her mother, "but he will not greet thee to-day, nor must thou greet him."

"What a strange, sad man is he!" said the child, as if speaking partly to herself. "In the dark nighttime he calls us to him! And in the deep forest, where only the old trees can hear, he talks with thee! But, here, in the sunny day, and among all the people, he knows us not!"

"Be quiet, Pearl! Thou understandest not these things," said her mother. "Think not now of the minister, but look about thee, and see how cheery is everybody's face to-day."

The crew of the vessel from the Spanish Main, who had come ashore to see the humors of Election Day were in the market place. They were rough-looking desperadoes, with sun-blackened faces, and an immensity of beard. Roger Chillingworth, the physician, was seen to enter the market-place in close and familiar talk with the commander of the questionable vessel.

After parting from the physician, the commander of the Bristol ship strolled idly through the market-place; until happening to approach the spot where Hester Prynne was standing, he appeared to recognize, and did not hesitate to address her. As was usually the case wherever Hester stood, a small vacant area, a sort of magic circle, had formed itself about her. It was a forcible type of the moral solitude in which the scarlet letter enveloped its fated wearer; partly by her own reserve, and partly by the instinctive, though no longer so unkindly, withdrawal of her fellow-creatures. Now, if never before, it answered a good purpose by enabling Hester and the seaman to speak together without risk of being overheard; and so changed was Hester Prynne's repute before the public, that the matron in town, most eminent for rigid morality, could not have held such intercourse with less result of scandal than herself.

"So, mistress," said the mariner, "I must bid the steward make ready one more berth than you bargained for! No fear of scurvy or ship fever this voyage. What with the ship's surgeon and this other doctor, our only danger will be from drug or pill; more by token, as there is a lot of apothecary's stuff aboard, which I traded for with a Spanish vessel."

"What mean you?" inquired Hester, startled more than she permitted to appear. "Have you another passenger?"

"Why, know you not," cried the shipmaster, "that this physician here, Chillingworth he calls himself, is minded to try my cabin-fare with you? Ay, ay, you must have known it; for he tells me he is of your party, and a close friend to the gentleman you spoke of, he that is in peril from these sour old Puritan rulers."

"They know each other well, indeed," replied Hester, with a mien of calmness, though in the utmost consternation. "They have long dwelt together."

Nothing further passed between the mariner and Hester Prynne. But at that instant she beheld old Roger Chillingworth himself, standing in the remotest corner of the market-place and smiling on her; a smile which, across the wide and bustling square, and through all the talk and laughter, and various thoughts, moods, and interests of the crowd, conveyed secret and fearful meaning.

CHAPTER 22: THE PROCESSION

Soon the head of the procession showed itself, with a slow and stately march, turning a corner, and making its way across the market-place. First came the music. It comprised a variety of instruments, perhaps imperfectly adapted to one another, and played with no great skill; but yet attaining the great object for which the harmony of drum and clarion addresses itself to the multitude and more heroic air to the scene of life that passes before the eye. Little Pearl at first clapped her hands, but then lost for an instant the restless agitation that had kept her in a continual effervescence throughout the morning; she gazed silently, and seemed to be borne upward like a floating sea-bird on the long heaves and swells of sound. But she was brought back to her former mood by the shimmer of the sunshine on the weapons and bright armor of the military company, which followed after the music, and formed the honorary escort of the procession.

The men of civil eminence, who came immediately behind the military escort, were better worth a thoughtful observer's eye. These primitive statesmen, therefore, Bradstreet, Endicott, Dudley, Bellingham, and their compeers, who were elevated to power by the early choice of the people, seem to have been not often brilliant, but distinguished by a ponderous sobriety, rather than activity of intellect. They had fortitude and self-reliance, and in time of difficulty or peril stood up for the welfare of the state like a line of cliffs against a tempestuous tide.

Next in order to the magistrates came the young and eminently distinguished divine, from whose lips the religious discourse of the anniversary was expected. His was the profession at that era in which intellectual ability displayed itself far more than in political life.

It was the observation of those who beheld him now, that never, since Mr. Dimmesdale first set his foot on the New England shore, had he exhibited such energy as was seen in the gait and air with which he kept his pace in the procession. There was no feebleness of step as at other times; his frame was not bent, nor did his hand rest ominously upon his heart. Yet, if the clergyman were rightly viewed, his strength seemed not of the body. It might be spiritual and imparted to him by angelical ministrations. There was his body, moving onward, and with an unaccustomed force. But where was his mind? Far and deep in its own region, busying itself, with preternatural activity, to marshal a procession of stately thoughts that were soon to issue thence; and so he saw nothing, heard nothing, knew nothing of what was around him; but the spiritual element took up the feeble frame and carried it along, unconscious of the burden, and converting it to spirit like itself. Men of uncommon intellect, who have grown morbid, possess this occasional power of mighty effort, into which they throw the life of many days and then are lifeless for as many more.

Hester Prynne, gazing steadfastly at the clergyman, felt a dreary influence come over her, but wherefore or whence she knew not, unless that he seemed so remote from her own sphere, and utterly beyond her reach. One glance of recognition she had imagined must needs pass between them. She thought of the dim forest where, sitting hand-in-hand, they had mingled their sad and passionate talk with the melancholy murmur of the brook. How deeply had they known each other then! And was this the man? She hardly knew him now! He, moving proudly past, enveloped as it were, in the rich music, with the procession of majestic and venerable fathers. Her spirit sank with the idea that all must have been a delusion, and that, vividly as she had dreamed it, there could be no real bond betwixt the clergyman and herself.

Pearl either saw and responded to her mother's feelings, or herself felt the remoteness and intangibility that had fallen around the minister. While the procession passed, the child was uneasy. When the whole had gone by, she looked up into Hester's face.

"Mother," said she, "was that the same minister that kissed me by the brook?"

"Hold thy peace, dear little Pearl!" whispered her mother. "We must not always talk in the marketplace of what happens to us in the forest."

"I could not be sure that it was he; so strange he looked," continued the child. "Else I would have run to him, and bid him kiss me now, before all the people. What would the minister have said, mother?"

"What should he say, Pearl," answered Hester, "save that it was no time to kiss!"

In reference to Mr. Dimmesdale, a person whose eccentricities led her to do what few of the townspeople would have done; to begin a conversation with the wearer of the scarlet letter in public. It was Mistress Hibbins. As this ancient lady had the renown of being a principal actor in all the works of necromancy that were continually going forward, the crowd gave way before her, and seemed to fear the touch of her garment.

"Now, what mortal imagination could conceive it?" whispered the old lady confidentially to Hester. "Yonder divine man! That saint on earth, as the people uphold him to be! Who, now, that saw him pass in the procession, would think how little while it is since he went forth out of his study to take an airing in the forest! Aha! we know what that means, Hester Prynne! But truly, forsooth, I find it hard to believe him the same man. Couldst thou surely tell, Hester, whether he was the same man that encountered thee on the forest path?"

"Madam, I know not of what you speak," answered Hester Prynne.

"Fie, woman, fie!" cried the old lady, shaking her finger at Hester. "Dost thou think I have been to the forest so many times, and have yet no skill to judge who else has been there? I know thee, Hester, for I behold the token. Thou wearest it openly, so there need be no question about that. But this minister! Let me tell thee in thine ear! When the Black Man sees one of his own servants, signed and sealed, so shy of owning to the bond as is the Reverend Mr. Dimmesdale, he hath a way of ordering matters so that the mark shall be disclosed, in open daylight, to the eyes of all the world! What is that the minister seeks to hide, with his hand always over his heart? Ha, Hester Prynne?"

"What is it, good Mistress Hibbins?" eagerly asked little Pearl. "Hast thou seen it?"

"No matter, darling!" responded Mistress Hibbins, making Pearl a profound reverence. "Thou thyself wilt see it, one time or another. They say, child, thou art of the lineage of the Prince of Air! Wilt thou ride with me some fine night to see thy father? Then thou shalt know wherefore the minister keeps his hand over his heart!" Laughing so shrilly that all the market-place could hear her, the weird old gentlewoman took her departure.

By this time the preliminary prayer had been offered in the meeting-house, and the accents of the Reverend Mr. Dimmesdale were heard commencing his discourse. Hester Prynne listened with such intenseness, and sympathized so intimately, that the sermon had throughout a meaning for her, entirely apart from its indistinguishable words. And yet, majestic as the voice sometimes became, there was forever in it an essential character of plaintiveness. A loud or low expression of anguish, the whisper, or the shriek, as it might be conceived, of suffering humanity, that touched a sensibility in every bosom! At times this deep strain of pathos was all that could be heard, and scarcely heard sighing amid a desolate silence. But even when the minister's voice grew high and commanding still, if the auditor listened intently, and for the purpose, he could detect the same cry of pain. What was it? The complaint of a human heart, sorrow-laden, perchance guilty, telling its secret, whether of guilt or sorrow, to the great heart of mankind; beseeching its sympathy or forgiveness, at every moment, in each accent, and never in vain! It was this profound and continual undertone that gave the clergyman his most appropriate power.

During all this time, Hester stood, statue-like, at the foot of the scaffold. If the minister's voice had not kept her there, there would, nevertheless, have been an inevitable magnetism in that spot, whence she dated the first hour of her life of ignominy. There was a sense within her that her whole orb of life, both before and after, was connected with this spot, as with the one point that gave it unity.

Little Pearl, meanwhile, had quitted her mother's side, and was playing at her own will about the market-place. She made the somber crowd cheerful by her erratic and glistening ray. Thence, with native audacity, but still with a reserve as characteristic, she flew into the midst of a group of mariners and they gazed wonderingly and admiringly at Pearl, as if a flake of the sea-foam had taken the shape of a little maid.

One of these seafaring men the shipmaster, indeed, who had spoken to Hester Prynne was so smitten with Pearl's aspect, that he attempted to lay hands upon her, with purpose to snatch a kiss. Finding it as impossible to touch her as to catch a humming-bird in the air, he took from his hat the gold chain that was twisted about it, and threw it to the child. Pearl immediately twined it around her neck and waist with such happy skill, that, once seen there, it became a part of her, and it was difficult to imagine her without it.

"Thy mother is yonder woman with the scarlet letter," said the seaman, "Wilt thou carry her a message from me?"

"If the message pleases me, I will," answered Pearl.

"Then tell her," rejoined he, "that I spake again with the black-a-visaged, hump shouldered old doctor, and he engages to bring his friend, the gentleman she wots of, aboard with him. So let thy mother take no thought, save for herself and thee. Wilt thou tell her this, thou witch-baby?"

Pursuing a zigzag course across the marketplace, the child returned to her mother, and communicated what the mariner had said. Hester's strong, calm steadfastly-enduring spirit almost sank, at last, on beholding this dark and grim countenance of an inevitable doom.

With her mind harassed by the terrible perplexity in which the shipmaster's intelligence involved her, she was also subjected to another trial. There were many people present from the country round about, who had often heard of the scarlet letter, and to whom it had been made terrific by a hundred false or exaggerated rumors, but who had never beheld it with their own bodily eyes. These, after exhausting other modes of amusement, now thronged about Hester Prynne with rude and boorish intrusiveness. At the final hour, when she was so soon to fling aside the burning letter, it had strangely become the centre of more remark and excitement, and was thus made to sear her breast more painfully, than at any time since the first day she put it on.

While Hester stood in that magic circle of ignominy, where the cunning cruelty of her sentence seemed to have fixed her forever, the admirable preacher was looking down from the sacred pulpit upon an audience whose very inmost spirits had yielded to his control. The sainted minister in the church! The woman of the scarlet letter in the marketplace! What imagination would have been irreverent enough to surmise that the same scorching stigma was on them both!

CHAPTER 23:
THE REVELATION OF THE SCARLET LETTER

The eloquent voice, on which the souls of the listening audience had been borne aloft as on the swelling waves of the sea, at length came to a pause. In a moment more the crowd began to gush forth from the doors of the church.

In the open air their rapture broke into speech. The street and the market-place absolutely babbled, from side to side, with applauses of the minister. According to their united testimony, never had man spoken in so wise, so high, and so holy a spirit, as he that spake this day. But, throughout it all, and through the whole discourse, there had been a certain deep, sad undertone of pathos, which could not be interpreted otherwise than as the natural regret of one soon to pass away. Yes; their minister whom they so loved had the foreboding of untimely death upon him, and would soon leave them in their tears. This idea of his transitory stay on earth gave the last emphasis to the effect which the preacher had produced; it was as if an angel, in his passage to the skies, had shaken his bright wings over the people for an instant and had shed down a shower of golden truths upon them.

Thus, there had come to the Reverend Mr. Dimmesdale an epoch of life more brilliant and full of triumph than any previous one, or than any which could hereafter be. He stood, at this moment, on the very proudest eminence of superiority. Such was the position which the minister occupied, as he bowed his head forward on the cushions of the pulpit at the close of his Election Sermon. Meanwhile Hester Prynne was standing beside the scaffold of the pillory, with the scarlet letter still burning on her breast!

Now was heard again the clamor of the music, and the measured tramp of the military escort issuing from the church door. The procession was to be marshaled thence to the town hall, where a solemn banquet would complete the ceremonies of the day.

Once more, therefore, the train of venerable and majestic fathers were seen moving through a broad pathway of the people, who drew back reverently, on either side, as the Governor and magistrates, the old and wise men, the holy ministers, and all that were eminent and renowned, advanced into the midst of them. When they were fairly in the marketplace, their presence was greeted by a shout. Never, from the soil of New England had gone up such a shout! Never, on New England soil had stood the man so honored by his mortal brethren as the preacher!

As the ranks of military men and civil fathers moved onward, all eyes were turned towards the point where the minister was seen to approach among them. The shout died into a murmur, as one portion of the crowd after another obtained a glimpse of him. How feeble and pale he looked, amid all his triumph! It seemed hardly the face of a man alive, with such a death-like hue: it was hardly a man with life in him, that tottered on his path so nervously, yet tottered, and did not fall!

The minister walked onward, if that movement could be so described, which rather resembled the wavering effort of an infant, with its mother's arms in view, outstretched to tempt him forward. And now, almost imperceptible as were the latter steps of his progress, he had come opposite the well-remembered and weather-darkened scaffold, where, long since, with all that dreary lapse of time between, Hester Prynne had encountered the world's ignominious stare. There stood Hester, holding little Pearl by the hand! And there was the scarlet letter on her breast! The minister here made a pause; although the music still played the stately and rejoicing march to which the procession moved. It summoned him onward but here he made a pause.

Bellingham, for the last few moments, had kept an anxious eye upon him. He now left his own place in the procession, and advanced to give assistance judging, from Mr. Dimmesdale's aspect that he must otherwise inevitably fall. The crowd, meanwhile, looked on with awe and wonder.

He turned towards the scaffold, and stretched forth his arms. "Hester," said he, "come hither! Come, my little Pearl!"

It was a ghastly look with which he regarded them; but there was something at once tender and strangely triumphant in it. The child, with the bird-like motion, which was one of her characteristics, flew to him, and clasped her arms about his knees. Hester Prynne, slowly, as if impelled by inevitable fate, and against her strongest will, likewise drew near, but paused before she reached him. At this instant old Roger Chillingworth thrust himself through the crowd, or, perhaps, so dark, disturbed, and evil was his look, he rose up out of some nether region, to snatch back his victim from what he sought to do! Be that as it might, the old man rushed forward, and caught the minister by the arm.

"Madman, hold! what is your purpose?" whispered he. "Wave back that woman! Cast off this child! All shall be well! Do not blacken your fame, and perish in dishonor! I can yet save you! Would you bring infamy on your sacred profession?"

"Ha, tempter! Me thinks thou art too late!" answered the minister, encountering his eye, fearfully, but firmly. "Thy power is not what it was! With God's help, I shall escape thee now!"

He again extended his hand to the woman of the scarlet letter.

"Hester Prynne," cried he, with a piercing earnestness, "in the name of Him, so terrible and so merciful, who gives me grace, at this last moment, to do what I withheld myself from doing seven years ago, come hither now, and twine thy strength about me! This wretched and wronged old man is opposing it with all his might. Hester, come! Support me up yonder scaffold."

The crowd was in a tumult. They beheld the minister, leaning on Hester's shoulder, and supported by her arm around him, approach the scaffold, and ascend its steps; while still the little hand of the sin-born child was clasped in his. Old Roger Chillingworth followed, as one intimately connected with the drama of guilt and sorrow in which they had all been actors, and well entitled, therefore to be present at its closing scene.

"Hadst thou sought the whole earth over," said he looking darkly at the clergyman, "there was no one place so secret, no high place nor lowly place, where thou couldst have escaped me, save on this very scaffold!"

"Thanks be to Him who hath led me hither!" answered the minister.

Yet he trembled, and turned to Hester, with an expression of doubt and anxiety in his eyes, not the less evidently betrayed, that there was a feeble smile upon his lips. "Is not this better," murmured he, "than what we dreamed of in the forest?"

"I know not! I know not!" she hurriedly replied. "Better? Yea; so we may both die, and little Pearl die with us!"

"For thee and Pearl, be it as God shall order," said the minister; "and God is merciful! Let me now do the will which He hath made plain before my sight. For, Hester, I am a dying man. So let me make haste to take my shame upon me!"

Partly supported by Hester Prynne, and holding one hand of little Pearl's, the Reverend Mr. Dimmesdale turned to the dignified and venerable rulers; to the holy ministers, who were his brethren; to the people, whose great heart was thoroughly appalled.

"People of New England!" cried he, with a voice that rose over them, high, solemn, and majestic, "behold me here, the one sinner of the world! I stand upon the spot where, seven years since, I should have stood! Lo, the scarlet letter which Hester wears! Ye have all shuddered at it! But there stood one in the midst of you, at whose brand of sin and infamy ye have not shuddered!"

It seemed, at this point, as if the minister must leave the remainder of his secret undisclosed. But he fought back the bodily weakness. He threw off all assistance, and stepped passionately forward a pace before the woman and the children.

"It was on him!" he continued, with a kind of fierceness; so determined was he to speak out the whole. "God's eye beheld it! The angels were forever pointing at it! The Devil knew it well, and fretted it continually with the touch of his burning finger! Now, at the death-hour, he stands up before you! He bids you look again at Hester's scarlet letter! He tells you, that, with all its mysterious horror, it is but the shadow of what he bears on his own breast, and that even this, his own red stigma, is no more than the type of what has seared his inmost heart! Stand any here that question God's judgment on a sinner! Behold! Behold, a dreadful witness of it!"

With a convulsive motion, he tore away the ministerial band from before his breast. It was revealed! But it were irreverent to describe that revelation. For an instant, the gaze of the horror-stricken multitude was concentrated on the ghastly miracle; while the minister stood, with a flush of triumph in his face, as one who, in the crisis of acutest pain, had won a victory. Then, down he sank upon the scaffold! Hester partly raised him, and supported his head against her bosom. Old Roger Chillingworth knelt down beside him, with a blank, dull countenance, out of which the life seemed to have departed.

"Thou hast escaped me!" he repeated more than once. "Thou hast escaped me!"

"May God forgive thee!" said the minister. "Thou, too, hast deeply sinned!" He withdrew his dying eyes from the old man, and fixed them on the woman and the child.

"My little Pearl," said he, feebly and there was a sweet and gentle smile over his face, as of a spirit sinking into deep repose; nay, now that the burden was removed, it seemed almost as if he would be sportive with the child, "dear little Pearl, wilt thou kiss me now? Thou wouldst not, yonder, in the forest! But now thou wilt?"

Pearl kissed his lips. A spell was broken. The great scene of grief, in which the wild infant bore a part had developed all her sympathies; and as her tears fell upon her father's cheek, they were the pledge that she would grow up amid human joy and sorrow, nor forever do battle with the world, but be a woman in it. Towards her mother, too, Pearl's errand as a messenger of anguish was fulfilled.

"Hester," said the clergyman, "farewell!"

"Shall we not meet again?" whispered she, bending her face down close to his. "Shall we not spend our immortal life together? Surely, surely, we have ransomed one another, with all this woe! Thou lookest far into eternity, with those bright dying eyes! Then tell me what thou seest!"

"Hush, Hester, hush!" said he, with tremulous solemnity. "The law we broke! It may be that when we forgot our God it was thenceforth vain to hope that we could meet hereafter, in an everlasting and pure reunion. God knows; and He is merciful! He hath proved his mercy, most of all, in my afflictions. By giving me this burning torture to bear upon my breast! By sending yonder dark and terrible old man, to keep the torture always at red-heat! By bringing me hither, to die this death of triumphant ignominy before the people! Had either of these agonies been wanting, I had been lost forever! Praised be His name! His will be done! Farewell!"

That final word came forth with the minister's expiring breath. The multitude, silent till then, broke out in a strange, deep voice of awe and wonder, which could not as yet find utterance, save in this murmur that rolled so heavily after the departed spirit.

CHAPTER 24: CONCLUSION

After many days, when time sufficed for the people to arrange their thoughts in reference to the foregoing scene, there was more than one account of what had been witnessed on the scaffold.

Most of the spectators testified to having seen, on the breast of the unhappy minister, a Scarlet Letter imprinted in the flesh. As regarded its origin there were various explanations. Some affirmed that the Reverend Mr. Dimmesdale, on the very day when Hester Prynne first wore her ignominious badge, had begun a course of penance by inflicting a hideous torture on himself. Others contended that the stigma had not been produced until a long time subsequent, when old Roger Chillingworth, being a potent necromancer, had caused it to appear, through the agency of magic and poisonous drugs. Others, again whispered their belief, that the awful symbol was the effect of the ever-active tooth of remorse, gnawing from the inmost heart outwardly, and at last manifesting Heaven's dreadful judgment by the visible presence of the letter.

It is singular, nevertheless, that certain persons, who were spectators of the whole scene, and professed never once to have removed their eyes from the Reverend Mr. Dimmesdale, denied that there was any mark whatever on his breast, more than on a new-born infant's. Neither, by their report, had his dying words acknowledged, nor even remotely implied, any, the slightest, connection on his part, with the guilt for which Hester Prynne had so long worn the scarlet letter. According to these highly-respectable witnesses, the minister, conscious that he was dying had desired, by yielding up his breath in the arms of that fallen woman, to express to the world how utterly nugatory is the choicest of man's own righteousness. After exhausting life in his efforts for mankind's spiritual good, he had made the manner of his death a parable, in order to impress on his admirers the mighty and mournful lesson, that, in the view of Infinite Purity, we are sinners all alike.

Nothing was more remarkable than the change which took place, almost immediately after Mr. Dimmesdale's death, in the appearance and demeanor of the old man known as Roger Chillingworth. All his strength and energy seemed at once to desert him. This unhappy man had made the very principle of his life to consist in the pursuit and systematic exercise of revenge. It is a curious subject of observation and inquiry, whether hatred and love be not the same thing at bottom. Each, in its utmost development, supposes a high degree of intimacy and heart-knowledge; each leaves the passionate lover, or the no less passionate hater, forlorn and desolate by the withdrawal of his subject. Philosophically considered, therefore, the two passions seem essentially the same, except that one happens to be seen in a celestial radiance, and the other in a dusky and lurid glow. In the spiritual world, the old physician and the minister may, unawares, have found their earthly stock of hatred and antipathy transmuted into golden love.

At old Roger Chillingworth's decease, which took place within the year, and by his last will and testament, of which Governor Bellingham and the Reverend Mr. Wilson were executors, he bequeathed a very considerable amount of property, both here and in England to little Pearl, the daughter of Hester Prynne.

So Pearl, the demon offspring, as some people up to that epoch persisted in considering her, became the richest heiress of her day in the New World. In no long time after the physician's death, the wearer of the scarlet letter disappeared, and Pearl along with her. The story of the scarlet letter grew into a legend. Its spell, however, was still potent, and kept the scaffold awful where the poor minister had died, and likewise the cottage by the sea-shore where Hester Prynne had dwelt. Near this latter spot, one afternoon some children were at play, when they beheld a tall woman in a gray robe approach the cottage-door. In all those years it had never once been opened; but either she unlocked it or the decaying wood and iron yielded to her hand, or she glided shadow-like through these impediments, and, at all events, went in.

On the threshold she paused, turned partly round, for perchance the idea of entering alone and all so changed, the home of so intense a former life, was more dreary and desolate than even she could bear. But her hesitation was only for an instant, though long enough to display a scarlet letter on her breast.

And Hester Prynne had returned, and taken up her long-forsaken shame! But where was little Pearl? If still alive she must now have been in the flush and bloom of early womanhood. None knew. But through the remainder of Hester's life there were indications that the recluse of the scarlet letter was the object of love and interest with some inhabitant of another land. Letters came, with armorial seals upon them, though of bearings unknown to English heraldry. In the cottage there were articles of comfort and luxury such as Hester never cared to use, but which only wealth could have purchased and affection have imagined for her. And once Hester was seen embroidering a baby-garment with such a lavish richness of golden fancy as would have raised a public tumult had any infant thus appareled, been shown to our sober-hued community.

In fine, the gossips of that day believed that Pearl was not only alive, but married, and happy, and mindful of her mother; and that she would most joyfully have entertained that sad and lonely mother at her fireside.

But there was a more real life for Hester Prynne, here, in New England, than in that unknown region where Pearl had found a home. Here had been her sin; here, her sorrow; and here was yet to be her penitence. She had returned, therefore, and resumed the symbol of which we have related so dark a tale. Never afterwards did it quit her bosom. But, in the lapse of the toilsome, thoughtful, and self-devoted years that made up Hester's life, the scarlet letter ceased to be a stigma which attracted the world's scorn and bitterness, and became a type of something to be sorrowed over, and looked upon with awe, yet with reverence too. And, as Hester Prynne had no selfish ends, nor lived in any measure for her own profit and enjoyment, people brought all their sorrows and perplexities, and besought her counsel, as one who had herself gone through a mighty trouble. She assured them, too, of her firm belief that, at some brighter period, when the world should have grown ripe for it, in Heaven's own time, a new truth would be revealed, in order to establish the whole relation between man and woman on a surer ground of mutual happiness.

So said Hester Prynne, and glanced her sad eyes downward at the scarlet letter. And, after many, many years, a new grave was delved, near an old and sunken one, in that burial-ground beside which King's Chapel has since been built. It was near that old and sunken grave, yet with a space between, as if the dust of the two sleepers had no right to mingle. Yet one tomb-stone served for both. All around, there were monuments carved with armorial bearings; and on this simple slab of slate there appeared the semblance of an engraved escutcheon. It bore a device, a herald's wording of which may serve for a motto and brief description of our now concluded legend; so somber is it, and relieved only by one ever-glowing point of light gloomier than the shadow:

"ON A FIELD, SABLE, THE LETTER A, GULES"

LIST OF MAIN CHARACTERS

Narrator – The narrator of The Scarlet Letter is described in the Custom House chapter. He used to work as the surveyor of the Salem Custom House a few hundred years after the events in the book. While working at the Custom House, the narrator discovered a manuscript in a neglected part of the building which tells the story of Hester Prynne. The narrator eventually loses his job at the Custom House and begins writing the work known as The Scarlet Letter. The narrator is never given a name in the book but it was known that Hawthorne had worked at a Custom House and the narrator is most likely a fictional version of himself.

Hester Prynne – Hester is the main character in the book and is the wearer of the scarlet letter. Before coming to America, she was married to Roger Chillingworth. Chillingworth sent her ahead to America and the plan was to follow here there. However, Chillingworth ended up being delayed to America and while waiting for him she had an affair with the young minister in town, Reverend Arthur Dimmesdale. The result of this affair was a daughter named Pearl. Hester needed to be a strong woman to endure the years of alienation and ridicule from her community. Towards the end of the book she gained a respect from the community in all the charity work she had performed. By being an outsider she was able to observe the community from a distance and thought of ways that society could improve itself, especially concerning the treatment of women.

Pearl – Hester's and Dimmesdale's daughter. Simply naming her daughter Pearl is symbolic enough as a pearl was thought to symbolize purity. The Pearl in the book is a moody and sometimes difficult to deal with. She has a mind of her own and lets the world know it. At the end of the book she is in essence freed from torment that her mother was forced to endure when Dimmesdale acknowledges her as his daughter and she kisses him on the lips. She ends up inheriting the fortune of Roger Chillingworth and by all accounts she leaves the community for a better life.

Roger Chillingworth – Chillingworth is Hester's actual husband. He is introduced in the book as Hester stands upon the scaffold. He tells Hester to keep their marriage a secret while he seeks to find out the truth behind who the father of Hester's daughter is. He lives his life from that point on for revenge and it slowly takes a toll on his life and his appearance. He disguises himself as a doctor based on his scholarly knowledge. He learned much of what he knows about medicine from being a captive of the Indians which was why he was delayed in reaching Hester in the community.

Reverend Arthur Dimmesdale – Dimmesdale is described as a young man in the book. He had an affair with Hester and was the father of Pearl. Hester couldn't hide fact that she committed adultery but Dimmesdale had a choice to confess or keep quiet. Not confessing his sin publicly may have been a worse fate than what Hester endured as his psychological torture caused him to develop a serious heart condition and led to an early death.

Reverend John Wilson – Wilson is the elder clergyman to Dimmesdale. Just like Governor Bellingham, Wilson typically follows a strict adherence to the Puritan rules but is swayed by the influence of Dimmesdale. His sermons are described as being harsher than Dimmesdale's as Wilson focuses on punishing sinners in the harshest of ways.

Governor Bellingham – Although a strict governor, Bellingham seems to go easy on Hester because he is influenced by Dimmesdale. After all, Bellingham could have taken Pearl away from her or even banished Hester from the community or worse. Strange that it may be, he is not aware that his own sister, Mistress Hibbins, is far worse than Hester in that she is a practicing witch.

Mistress Hibbins – Mistress Hibbins is the first person in the community, probably other than Chillingworth, to realize that something is amiss with Dimmesdale. It's obvious that she puts two and two together and realizes that Dimmesdale is the father of Pearl. She references "The Black Man" also known as Satan. She can be thought of to represent some type of hypocrisy in the Puritan community. After all, she is a practicing witch that is roaming the town with no questions asked yet Hester is the one singled out for her sin.

CHAPTER NOTES: WHAT YOU NEED TO KNOW

Introduction: The Custom House

- The narrator addresses the reader and describes how he came into knowing the story of Hester Prynne.
- Hawthorne did actually work in a Custom House so the narrator is most likely a fictional version of himself.
- The Custom House narration gives the book a historical feel and leads to the believability of the story.
- The Custom House is old and full of employees who don't do much actual work.
- One day the narrator found the manuscript describing the events in the book and the actual fabric scarlet letter A.
- The manuscripts were the work of Surveyor Jonathan Pue who collected the information about 100 years prior to the narrator finding them.
- The narrator debates about writing a book about the story that he found and if he is even an able enough writer to do it.
- The narrator wonders if his Puritan ancestors would approve of his work.
- In the end, the narrator loses his job and writes his novel.

Chapter 1: The Prison Door

- Chapter is short and sweet. The town has gathered to witness Hester coming out of the prison for the first time with her illegitimate baby.
- A wild rose bush grows on the side of the door. The rose bush was thought to be a way to bless criminals entering the prison as well as exiting the prison.

Chapter 2: The Market Place

- As punishment Hester is taken to a public area in the community, the market place, and required to stand on top of a scaffold for all to see.
- Some townspeople think Hester should be executed for her crime.

- In addition, Hester is required to wear a scarlet letter A. However, due to her amazing embroidery skills, she crafted the A to look beautiful and it doesn't go over well with some of the townspeople.
- Hester realizes that she will always be an outsider from this day forth.
- As the reality of the events hit her she squeezes her baby so tight that it starts to cry. At this point, her baby is about 3 months old.

Chapter 3: The Recognition

- Hester, still on the scaffold catches the eye of a white man with an Indian. When she sees the white man she squeezes the baby again so hard that it cries.
- The stranger asks a townsperson who Hester is and why she was on the scaffold. The stranger asks who the father is but no one knows the answer.
- We learn here that Hester used to live in Amsterdam and was married to a scholar. She came to Salem ahead of her husband but her husband never arrived.
- As Hester stares at the man she recognizes him from his deformities. Also, she is relieved that there are others around and that she is not alone with the man. The man makes a gesture to her to be quiet.
- John Wilson, an elder clergyman, asks Dimmesdale, the younger clergyman, to deal with Hester.
- Dimmesdale tells Hester to name the father. She refuses. The baby reaches out to Dimmesdale.
- Wilson then begins a long sermon about sin, focusing on the scarlet letter.
- Hester is then led back to the prison and a rumor spreads that the scarlet letter glows in the darkness.

Chapter 4: The Interview

- Hester, and more importantly, the baby are in poor health in the prison cell.
- The stranger arrives at the prison, introduces himself as Roger Chillingworth, and tells people that he is a doctor.

- Here we learn that Hester and Chillingworth were married.
- Alone with Chillingworth in the cell, Hester thinks that Chillingworth will kill her and the baby.
- Chillingworth asks for the name of the father. Hester refuses.
- Chillingworth then vows to seek out the father and begins his quest for vengence which will be his goal throughout the book.
- He makes Hester swear an oath to keep secret that they know each other and were married.
- Hester points out that this oath will be the ruin of her soul but Chillingworth tells her it won't be the ruin of her soul and implies that it will be the ruin of the father's.

Chapter 5: Hester at Her Needle

- Hester is released from prison. She now realizes that each day will be harder than the day before. She realizes that she is an outcast.
- Narrator questions why she even stays. Believes she stays for the father and because she is tied to the area.
- Her home is an abandoned cottage on the edge of town.
- She is a great seamstress and is able to make money with her needle.
- Everyone in town lets her know that she is a sinner and an outcast. The poor, who she helps, are mean to her. Even children make fun of her.
- She shows strength by not succumbing to the solitary anguish of her day to day life.
- She thinks the scarlet letter has given her insight into the hidden sins of others.
- This shows some hypocrisy within the community as her sin is public but other people's sins are hidden and the fact that they are hidden shows a false guise of purity.

Chapter 6: Pearl

- Pearl's name is a symbol by itself . It means, "purity". The name also symbolizes the price that her mother paid for her.
- Hester continually wonders if Pearl is evil or will be evil.

- While Hester wears plain clothes she dresses Pearl in the most beautiful dresses available.
- First thing that Pearl notices in her life is the scarlet letter.
- Pearl is continually drawn to the scarlet letter and lets Hester know about it. Pearl often throws flowers at the letter.
- Pearl tells Hester that she has no heavenly father.
- Hester recalls that some townspeople think that Pearl is a demon offspring.
- At the end of this chapter Pearl is about 3 years old.

Chapter 7: The Governor's Hall

- Hester travels to Governor Bellingham's house to deliver a pair of gloves.
- The other reason for the visit is that Bellingham has been talking about taking Pearl away from Hester.
- Pearl is dressed in a way that makes Hester think of the scarlet letter.
- While waiting inside Bellingham's house Hester sees her reflection in a suite of armor. Her reflection and the scarlet letter are distorted.

Chapter 8: The Elf-Child and the Minister

- Governor Bellingham, Reverend Wilson, Reverend Dimmesdale, and Roger Chillingworth finally arrive at Bellingham's house.
- Bellingham and Wilson think that Pearl should be taken from Hester.
- Dimmesdale convinces them to let Hester keep Pearl.
- Upon hearing this, Chillingworth grows more suspicious of Dimmesdale.
- While leaving, Hester and Pearl meet Bellingham's sister, Mistress Hibbins. Mistress Hibbins is later executed as a witch.
- Hibbins asks Hester if she will go with her to the forest to meet the Black Man (aka Satan).
- Hester says that if they had taken Pearl she would have gone. This is one instance in which Pearl has saved her mother.

Chapter 9: The Leech

- Leech is another name for a doctor during the time-period. This was due to the doctor's reliance on leeches as a treatment.
- Because of Dimmesdale's health, Chillingworth was originally thought of as a miracle by the townspeople. Their minister was in trouble and here arrives a doctor.
- Chillingworth soon becames Dimmesdale's physician.
- After awhile the two move in together so that Chillingworth can watch over his patient's every move.
- Towards the end of the chapter the townspeople begin to notice a change in Chillingworth's appearance. He has grown uglier and begins to look evil.

Chapter 10: The Leech and His Patient

- Chillingworth picks herbs from a grave and tells Dimmesdale that the herbs grew out of a secret in the dead man's heart.
- Chillingworth constantly questions Dimmesdale. Chillingworth tells Dimmesdale that he needs to disclose everything in his soul; every secret.
- Dimmesdale gets upset about this and storms off but is quick to apologize and returns under the care of Chillingworth.
- While Dimmesdale is sleeping, Chillingworth touches his chest and opens his shirt. Dimmesdale shudders and Chillingworth is now certain that Dimmesdale is the father of Pearl.

Chapter 11: The Interior of a Heart

- Chapter 11 is about the inner torment Dimmesdale goes through each day because of his secret.
- He imagines telling everyone. He actually tells the people at his church that he is a sinner but they only revere him more.
- He performs vigils where he fasts and sees visions in an attempt to purify his soul.

Chapter 12: The Minister's Vigil

- During one of Dimmesdale's vigils, he stumbles up the scaffold where Hester stood with Pearl. At this point in the story it is about 7 years since the day Hester first climbed up the scaffold.
- Dimmesdale cries out but it is midnight and no one hears him.
- He sees Hester and Pearl and calls them up to stand with him.
- Hester had been helping at the beside of Governor Winthrop who had just died.
- A meteor is seen and it lights up the night sky. The townspeople will say it lit up the sky with an A for Angel for Governor Winthrop. Dimmesdale thinks that it is shedding light on his sin.
- During the meteor Chillingworth is seen staring at the trio on the scaffold. People points at him. Dimmesdale admits that he fears him to Hester and yet still returns home with him.

Chapter 13: Another View of Hester

- Hester is shocked to see the terrible shape that Dimmesdale is in.
- Dimmesdale needs help and Hester decides that she must help him.
- 7 years have passed since she was on the scaffold. The women in the community now recognize Hester as a "Sister of Mercy". She helps those in need.
- Some of the women now began to think that the scarlet letter stood for Able.
- The men in the community are a little slower to forgive.
- Hester's hard life has caused her to lose the beauty that she once had. She cuts her hair short or covers it up and wears plain clothes. She is described as cold.
- Hester questions the treatment that women receive in society.
- Hester also wonders if she is to blame for Dimmesdale's health for not telling him about Chillingworth.

Chapter 14: Hester and the Physician

- Hester finds Chillingworth and tells Pearl to go play.

- Chillingworth tells Hester that a magistrate was thinking about letter her take off the scarlet letter.
- Hester says that if she is worthy it will fall off by itself.
- Hester notices an evil change in Chillingworth and thinks she is to blame for this change.
- Chillingworth sees his reflection while he is talking to Hester and is surprised at how he looks.
- Chillingworth admits that he is evil but that Hester is to blame.
- Hester tells Chillingworth that she is going to tell Dimmesdale the truth about him.
- Chillingworth tells her to go ahead and do it. He says, "Let the black flower blossom as it may!"

Chapter 15: Hester and Pearl

- Hester realizes that she hates Chillingworth and she wonders how she could ever have been married to him.
- Pearls comes back to her mother's side dressed up with seaweed to look like a mermaid. She even made a green letter A.
- Pearl asks what the scarlet letter is. She asks if it has anything to do with Dimmesdale.
- Hester debates telling Pearl the trust but decides against it. It seems that Hester still is trying to protect Pearl's innocence.
- Pearl continues to drive Hester crazy by continually asking what the letter means.

Chapter 16: A Forest Walk

- Hester seeks out Dimmesdale and in doing so walks through the forest with Pearl.
- Pearl laughs at how the sunshine seems to avoid Hester in the forest.
- Pearl says that Mistress Hibbins told her about the "Black Man" (Satan).
- Pearl asks if Hester has ever met him.
- Hester says that she has and the scarlet letter is his mark.
- They both see Dimmesdale approaching. He has his hand over his heart.

- Pearl asks if it has anything to do with the "Black Man".

Chapter 17: The Pastor and His Parishioner

- Hester and Dimmesdale talk in the woods.
- Dimmesdale says that he is in torment. He wishes he had someone, friend or enemy, who could see him for what he is.
- Hester tells him that he does have an enemy, Chillingworth.
- Hester tells him the truth about Chillingworth.
- Dimmesdale first says that he can never forgive Hester for this.
- Hester pleads for forgiveness and eventually Dimmesdale forgives her.
- They both admit that the feelings they have for each other are still there.
- Dimmesdale asks how he can ever go back and live with Chillingworth now that he knows the truth.
- Hester says that they should just leave the town and start a new life together.

Chapter 18: A Flood of Sunshine

- Dimmesdale debates leaving town with Hester.
- Hester persuades him to go.
- Once the decision is made Dimmesdale feel relieved and rejuvenated.
- Hester takes off the scarlet letter and takes off her formal cap to let her hair down. All of her beauty that was lost now returned.
- Hester calls Pearl in order for them to meet as father and daughter for the first time.

Chapter 19: The Child at the Brookside

- Dimmesdale says that he was always afraid that people would find out that he is the father of Pearl because they share a resemblance.
- Pearl reaches the edge of the brook that separates her from her parents and stops.

- She notices that Hester does not wear her scarlet letter, points at the place where it usually is on Hester, and starts screaming.
- Hester gets the letter and puts it back on.
- Pearl then jumps over the brook and kisses her mother and the letter.
- Pearl asks if Dimmesdale will walk back with them to the town. In other words, will he admit the truth to the townspeople?
- Hester says not at this time.
- Pearl then wants nothing to do with Dimmesdale. He kisses Pearl on the forehead but she washes it off in the brook.

Chapter 20: The Minister in a Maze

- As the minister heads back alone to the town we learn that Hester and Dimmesdale have agreed to go back to England.
- There is a ship that will sail just after the Election Sermon that Dimmesdale is going to give. He thinks this is the perfect time to end his career in town.
- As he makes his way back to the town he feels himself full of energy.
- Once he arrives in town he notices things are the same and yet something has changed. It the minister who himself has undergone a change.
- He feels sudden urges to do strange and evil things. One of them is to say blasphemous things to one of his elderly deacons.
- He runs into Mistress Hibbins who somehow knows he was in the forest. She tells him that next time he should let her know as she knows Satan.
- Dimmesdale realizes that in agreeing to flee town he has made a bargain with the devil and that bargain is what has led to these sudden urges.
- Dimmesdale makes it home and runs into Chillingworth. Even though they both know, in truth, that they are enemies neither of them bring up the subject. Chillingworth asks Dimmesdale if he wants medicine and Dimmesdale refuses.
- Dimmesdale then sits down and works all night on his farewell sermon.

Chapter 21: The New England Holiday

- A new governor was to receive his office so the town gathered in the marketplace and made it a holiday.
- Hester resumed her coldness in public but was thinking that soon she'd be rid of the scarlet letter and this town.
- Hester notices that Chillingworth was talking to the captain of the boat that was going to take them to England.
- The captain then comes over to Hester and tells her that Chillingworth is going to be coming with them.
- Hester sees Chillingworth smiling in a remote corner of the marketplace.

Chapter 22: The Procession

- The parade starts which will eventually lead to Dimmesdale giving an election sermon and the new governor being appointed to office.
- As Dimmesdale walks through the marketplace the townspeople are amazed at how much energy he seems to have. However, it seems to rise from a spiritual place as his body doesn't appear to have the strength to accomplish what he is doing.
- Once Hester sees Dimmesdale she is overcome with a bad feeling of what is to come. In fact, she hardly recognizes him. Even Pearl asks if that is the same man that kissed her in the forest.
- Mistress Hibbins walks up to Hester and says that she knows Dimmesdale took a walk in the forest. She asks Hester what it is that Dimmesdale is hiding.
- Hester doesn't answer. Mistress Hibbins says that it will come out sooner or later.
- Dimmesdale begins his final election sermon. As Hester listened she could hear a touch of sorrow or sadness in his voice.
- The captain of the ship sees Pearl and asks her to tell her mother this: Chillingworth is going to bring Dimmesdale onto the ship.
- Hester continues to feel an impending doom about what is going to happen.

Chapter 23: The Revelation of the Scarlet Letter

- After Dimmesdale finishes his sermon the townspeople mingle around and talk about how this was his most amazing sermon yet.
- The townspeople also think that Dimmesdale is probably going to die soon based on his health.
- As Dimmesdale walks through the crowd this time his energy seems to have vanished. He struggles with each step.
- Dimmesdale reaches the scaffold and climbs up the steps. He motions for Hester and Pearl to join him.
- Chillingworth steps forward and tells Dimmesdale not to do it. Chillingworth says he can save Dimmesdale. Dimmesdale tells Chillingworth to leave him alone.
- Hester, Pearl, Dimmesdale, and Chillingworth now all stand on the scaffold with Hester supporting Dimmesdale.
- Dimmesdale address the town and reveals the truth. He tears open his shirt and reveals his chest. Most of the townspeople will later agree that there was a scarlet letter on his chest.
- Chillingworth says Dimmesdale has escaped him.
- Pearl kisses Dimmesdale on the lips. A gesture which meant that she accepted him as her father and would be accepted by the world.
- Hester asks Dimmesdale if they will meet in heaven. Dimmesdale says that because of their sin he doesn't think so. But God knows and everything that has happened to him has been for the good as it has saved him.
- Dimmesdale then dies.

Chapter 24: Conclusion

- The townspeople talk about what has occurred. Most agree that they saw a scarlet letter on Dimmesdale's chest. However, how it came to be on his chest is debatable.
- Some think that he put it on his own chest. Others think that Chillingworth somehow did it. And other think that it was the result of his inner torment that produced it.

- Some townspeople say that there was no mark at all. They say that Dimmesdale never admitted to anything and that he did what he did as a lesson and to help a fallen woman.
- Chillingworth dies within a year of Dimmesdale and he leaves his fortune to Pearl.
- Pearl becomes the richest heiress in the New World.
- Shortly after Chillingworth's death Hester and Pearl leave the town.
- Hester returns many years later and goes back to living in her cottage.
- The rumor is that Pearl is alive and married as Hester frequently received mail and was once seen making a baby-garment for someone.
- The townspeople go to Hester for help with their sorrows and problems.
- Hester says that at some point the world will re-establish a mutual relationship between men and women.
- Hester dies and is buried in the same tomb as Dimmsdale but not right next to him.
- The epitaph reads, in other words, "The scarlet letter A".

SAMPLE QUIZZES
Quiz 1

1. What is the narrator's purpose in the Custom-House introduction to the novel?
    A. He describes the moral side of adultery
    B. he describes how he "discovered" the manuscript
    C. he just wanted to make an extremely boring opening
    D. he describes how much fun it is to work in a Custom House

2. What century is the story set?
    A. The nineteenth century
    B. The seventeenth century
    C. The fourteenth century
    D. The eighteenth century

3. Who tells Dimmesdale that he must "deal" with Hester when she is first on the scaffold at the beginning of the book?
    A. Reverend Wilson
    B. Governor Winthrop
    C. Pearl
    D. Mistress Hibbins

4. Where do Hester and Chillingworth live before coming to America?
    A. Paris
    B. Ireland
    C. Sweden
    D. Amsterdam

5. Why was Chillingworth delayed in arriving to the town?
    A. He had too much business to deal with at home
    B. He was just a slow traveler
    C. He kept stopping wherever he went
    D. He was a captive of Indians

6. What city does the story of Hester take place in?
    A. New York
    B.' Hartford
    C. Boston
    D. Charlotte

7. How is Hester able to make money?
 A. She's a poet
 B. She's a farmer
 C. She's a seamstress
 D. She doesn't make money

8. What must Hester always wear on her chest?
 A. A scarlet letter "A"
 B. A scarlet letter "C"
 C. The word "Adultery"
 D. The word "Sin"

9. Who does Pearl reach for as a baby when Hester is first on the scaffold?
 A. Chillingworth
 B. Dimmesdale
 C. Mistress Hibbins
 D. No one

10. Why is Hester relieved that when she sees Chillingworth for the first time there is a crowd of people between them?
 A. She's afraid of what he will do to her
 B. She thinks that the crowd will help him as he has traveled far
 C. She's not sure who he is
 D. She thinks he's a mirage

11. What does Chillingworth pretend to be?
 A. A doctor
 B. An Indian
 C. A governor from England
 D. A member of the royal family

12. Who is Pearl's real father?
 A. Chillingworth
 B. Dimmesdale
 C. Chillingworth's brother
 D. No one knows

13. What does Pearl do when Dimmesdale kisses her on the forehead in the forest?
- A. She blushes
- B. She screams
- C. She runs and dances in the brook
- D. She washes her forehead off in the brook

14. Who persuades Governor Bellingham and Reverend Wilson to let Hester keep her child, Pearl?
- A. Chillingworth
- B. Mistress Hibbins
- C. Dimmesdale
- D. No one, they end up taking Pearl for awhile

15. How does Pearl finally acknowledge that Dimmesdale is her father?
- A. She kisses him on the lips
- B. She calls him, "Dad"
- C. She tells everyone that he is the one
- D. She jumps on him

Quiz 2

1. What does Reverend Dimmesdale do throughout the book?
- A. Places his hand over his heart
- B. Performs science experiments
- C. Places his hand over his eyes
- D. Picks herbs and flowers

2. What is the first thing that Pearl fixates on as a baby?
- A. Her mother's eyes
- B. The scarlet letter
- C. Her mother's hands
- D. The prison door

3. Mistress Hibbins is thought to be a what?
- A. A saint
- B. A witch
- C. A doctor
- D. A farmer

4. Who is known as the Leech?
A. Chillingworth
B. Dimmesdale
C. Hester
D. Pearl

5. How does Chillingworth come to realize who the father of Pearl is?
A. He never knows who it is
B. Hester tells him
C. Mistress Hibbins tells him
D. He becomes Dimmedale's doctor and realizes the secret over time

6. What happens when Hester, Pearl, and Dimmesdale are on the scaffold for the first time together?
A. Everyone sees them
B. They laugh and dance in circles
C. An earthquake hits
D. A meteor lights up the sky and earth

7. How do the townspeople interpret the image displayed in the sky by the meteor?
A. They see an "A" for angel
B. They didn't notice the meteor
C. They see an image of Dimmesdale
D. They see an image of Satan

8. What does Hester say when she learns that the magistrates might let her take off the scarlet letter?
A. She says it's about time
B. She doesn't say anything to it
C. She says that only God can remove the letter
D. She takes the letter off

9. What does Pearl do when she sees Hester without the scarlet letter on in the forest?
A. She runs away
B. She dances in the brook
C. She points at her and begins to scream and cry
D. She jumps into the arms of Dimmesdale

10. What happens to Hester when she takes off the scarlet letter and lets her hair down in the forest?
  A. Her skin flushes with beauty
  B. She realizes that she is going bald
  C. She loses her cap
  D. She loses the scarlet letter

11. Hester convinces Dimmesdale to do what while they are in the forest?
  A. Tell the townspeople the truth
  B. Leave town with her and start a new life
  C. Kill Chillingworth
  D. Become a monk

12. Besides Chillingworth, who else guesses that Dimmesdale is hiding a secret?
  A. Bellingham
  B. Wilson
  C. Mistress Hibbins
  D. No one else thinks he is hiding anything

13. After many years what do the townspeople begin to think that the letter "A" that Hester must wear stands for?
  A. Another
  B. Average
  C. Able
  D. Nothing more than Adultery

14. What does Dimmesdale do to punish himself for his sins?
  A. Vigils and fasting
  B. He runs marathons
  C. He cooks meals for the town
  D. He helps the sick

15. In the end, Dimmesdale says that God has saved him, but how?
  A. By causing him to bear a burning tortuous secret
  B. By bringing Chilllingworth to torture him
  C. By bringing Dimmesdale to die in front of his people after confessing
  D. All of the above

Quiz Answers

Quiz 1:

1. B
2. B
3. A
4. D
5. D
6. C
7. C
8. A
9. B
10. A
11. A
12. B
13. D
14. C
15. A

Quiz 2:

1. A
2. B
3. B
4. A
5. D
6. D
7. A
8. C
9. C
10. A
11. B
12. C
13. C
14. A
15. D

Made in the USA
Lexington, KY
02 September 2018